This novel is ent
The names, charac
are the work of the

Any resemblance oi act relating to any
persons, living or dead, locations or
events involving them, is entirely alleged
or coincidental.

Published by BSA Publishing 2021 who
assert the right that no part of this
publication may be reproduced, stored in
a retrieval system or transmitted by any
means without the prior permission of the
publishers.

1

THE PALMER CASES
BACKGROUND

Justin Palmer started off on the beat as a London policeman in the late 1980s and is now Detective Chief Superintendent Palmer running the Serial Murder Squad from New Scotland Yard.

Not one to pull punches, or give a hoot for political correctness if it hinders his enquiries Palmer has gone as far as he will go in the Met. and he knows it. Master of the one line put down and slave to his sciatica he can be as nasty or as nice as he likes.

The early 2000's was a time of re-awakening for Palmer as the Information Technology revolution turned forensic science, communication and information gathering skills upside down. In 2012 realising the value of this revolution to crime solving Palmer co-opted Detective Sergeant Gheeta Singh, a young British Asian, working in the Met's Cyber Crime Unit into his team. DS Singh has a degree in IT and was given the go ahead to update Palmer's department with all the computer hard and software she wanted, most of which she wrote herself, and some of which is, shall we say, of a grey area when it comes to privacy laws and accessing certain databases!

Together with their civilian computer clerk called Claire, nicknamed 'JCB' by the team because she keeps on digging, they take on the serial killers of the UK. If more help is needed in a case Gheeta calls on a select number of officers in other departments who have worked with Palmer before and can't wait to do so again.

On the personal front Palmer has been married to his 'princess', or Mrs P. as she is known to everybody, for nearly forty years. The romance blossomed after the young DC Palmer arrested most of her family who were a bunch of South London petty villains in the 90's. They have four children and eight grandchildren, a nice house in Dulwich Village and a faithful dog called Daisy. His one nemesis is his next door neighbour Benji, real name Benjamin Courtney-Smythe, a portly, single, ex-advertising executive in his late fifties who has taken early retirement and now has, in Palmer's estimation, too much time on his hands and too much money in his pocket. Benji has a new car every year plus at least two cruise holidays a year to exotic parts; he wears designer label clothes befitting a much younger man, a fake tan, enough gold jewellery to interest the Hatton

Garden Safe Deposit Heist gang and all topped off with his thinning hair scooped into a ponytail: also befitting a much younger man. Benji has a habit of bringing calamities into Palmer's settled home life.

Palmer is also unsure about Benji's sexuality, as his mincing walk and the very female way of flapping his hands to illustrate every word cast doubts in Palmer's mind. Not that that worries Palmer, who is quite at ease in the multi-gender world of today. Of course, he will never admit it, but the main grudge he holds against Benji is that before Benji's arrival in the quiet suburb of Dulwich Village, Palmer had been the favourite amongst the ladies of the Women's Institute, the Bridge Club, the Church Flower Arrangers and the various other clubs catering for ladies of a certain age; but now Benji has usurped Palmer's fan base, and when he stood for, and was elected to, the local council on a mandate to reopen the library and bring back the free bus pass for pensioners Benji's popularity soared and their fluttering eyelashes turned away from Palmer and settled in his direction.

Gheeta Singh is twenty six and lives in a fourth floor Barbican apartment in London. Her parents arrived on these shores as refugees fleeing from Idi Amin's Uganda in the 1970's. Her father and brothers have built up a large computer parts supply company in which it was assumed Gheeta would take an active role on graduating from University with her IT degrees. However she had other ideas on her career path, and also on the arranged marriage her mother and aunt still try to coerce her into. Gheeta has two loves, police work and technology, and thanks to Palmer she has her dream job.

Combining the old 'coppers nose' and 'gut feelings' of Palmer with the modern IT skills of DS Singh the two make an unlikely but successful crime solving pair. As the name of the squad suggests, all their cases involve serial killings and twist and turn through red herrings and hidden clues alike keeping the reader in suspense until the very end.

****

LAPTOPS CAN KILL

DAY 1

'What have you got, Harry?' Nineteen year old George Lane sat back in the rickety old chair and brushed his long black hair back from his eyes with one hand, the other held his cards close to his chest.

'Two Kings,' his younger brother by two years Harry, thought he had a good hand.

He was wrong. George smiled a winning smile and laid his cards face up on the coffee table: an Ace and a Queen.

'Shit.' Harry threw down his pair of Kings and slumped dejectedly back in his chair that gave out a warning creak that its upright days were probably numbered. He gave his crew cut a scratch and rubbed his eyes. 'I reckon you've marked these cards, new deck next time.'

'All mine, come to daddy,' George picked up the banknotes from the table and put them into his jacket pocket. He stood up and stretched and looked around the room. 'This place is the pits. Look at it, it's 2021 not 1950. I vote we get our own place and let the council do whatever they want with this pigsty. Hasn't had a lick of paint for decades – none of the estate has. We can afford a decent place.'

'We can,' said Harry. 'No problem with the money. But you know as well as I do that if we do that then the probation service will want to know how we can afford it, and I don't think they'd appreciate being told 'by nicking stuff', do you?'

Their cousin Fred Smith was sitting on the old sofa that had also seen better days reading the paper. He was two years older than George and had the same family features as the brothers, bright eyes, black hair and like them was dressed casually in a light weight jacket and jeans. The only difference was he wore glasses that he removed and slipped into a top pocket, 'Come on, never mind about moving flats – we need to move our backsides. It's getting dark outside and the car parks will be busy with evening shoppers – work calls.' He stood and dropped the paper onto the coffee table scattering the playing cards. 'We might find another laptop left in full view on a car seat just begging to be lifted.'

George sat back and was serious, 'I don't think so, that was a once in a lifetime stroke of luck nicking that particular laptop, Mr Robert Day is going to have to pay a lot of dosh to get that back.'

Harry wasn't happy. 'I reckon we should chuck it in a skip – getting into dangerous waters with that. Day wouldn't want the info on it to get out in the open, no way. It's bloody dynamite!'

George shrugged. 'Well, if he pays us enough it won't get out, will it?'

'Just you think about it, George,' said Harry, sounding a note of caution. 'A list of bent coppers in the Met and how much Day pays them, amounts, dates and names. Let's face it, Day's not small fry is he, eh? He's a *Mr Big,* and he's not going to be very happy with us nicking his laptop, is he?'

George sighed and rolled his eyes. 'I told you before, don't worry. Sammy's going to sort it on the quiet, do it all through a third party, Day won't know it was us that stole it.'

The letterbox on the front door of Flat 62 on the sixth floor of Attlee House, The Bevan Estate, East Ham rattled loudly.

'Hopefully that's Sammy with a big wad of cash,' said Fred, leaving the room to open the door.

George patted Harry on the shoulder. 'Don't worry, Harry. Nobody knows we are the ones who lifted it, so we can negotiate a price at arm's length using a go-between.'

Fred came back in. His left arm was being twisted up his back and Jerry Houseman held a gun with a silencer fitted to the side of his head. Trevor Black followed them in.

Trevor Black was a fixer, somebody that those in the criminal underground paid to sort out things for them rather than get involved themselves; sort out things like removing competitors for good, and breaking limbs as a warning to leave the area. Black looked every inch a successful businessman, which in his sphere of business he was, silk cloth dark blue suit, matching shirt and tie, black polished brogues and his dark hair slicked back not a strand out of place. Jerry Houseman was Black's partner; just as nasty but the one of the pair who thinks things through first and makes sure there's a good gap between their 'jobs' and no obvious clues pointing at them. Jerry was also wearing a suit, the trouser creases were not as sharp as Black's but he wouldn't warrant a second look in a crowd, which was just what Jerry hoped. Blend in and be inconspicuous, the opposite to Black. They probably should have been named Chalk and Cheese not Black and Houseman. They were of course well known to the police, and now in their early sixties, they had led a charmed life as far as arrests were concerned, with neither being tapped for murder; that 'charmed life' made secure by any witnesses to their actions knowing only too well that to talk or point a finger towards the pair would bring an immediate violent reaction on themselves and their families. *Omerta* reigned when Black and Houseman were concerned.

Black smiled at the boys. 'Well, well, well, look who we have here – the young Lane brothers, George and Harry. We met your cousin Fred here at the door.'

George and Harry went to stand up, a mask of fear on their faces. Trevor Black raised an open hand towards them. 'Stay where you are, gentlemen. Do not move and do not say a word.' He nodded towards Jerry Houseman who pushed Fred violently down onto the sofa.

'Gentlemen,' Black continued as he took a gun from his pocket and purposely in full view slowly screwed on a silencer. 'You have something that doesn't belong to you.' He laughed. 'No doubt fucking little tea leaves like you three have lots of things that don't belong to you, but this item is very dear to a client of ours who would like it back. He would like it back now. You see, I'm afraid you chose the wrong car when you broke into the black Range Rover in Morrison's car park two nights ago.'

He turned to Houseman and spoke in a sarcastic way. 'I think it quite deplorable in this day and age that our client's wife can't even go into a supermarket to purchase items without a team of little street thieves robbing his car – quite deplorable. Don't you agree, Mr Houseman?'

Houseman nodded in agreement. 'I do, Mr Black, quite deplorable.'

Black turned back to the boys. 'A few enquiries in the right circles as to who these reprobates could be, and three names and an address kept popping up. Guess whose names, and which address?' His voice hardened. 'One laptop please, gentleman. I want it now.' He held out an open hand.

'What's the reward?' Fred asked, hoping a show of bravado might work. 'We know what's on it – gotta be worth a good bung to get that back.'

'So you've had a good look, have you?' Black raised his eyebrows. 'Been a bit nosey have you?'

'Yeah, and that type of information has got to be worth a good reward to get back. If the cops get hold of it your client's a goner.'

'And who is my client?' Black asked quietly, part of him hoping the boys didn't know.

'Robert Day,' Fred said, hoping that knowing who owned the laptop would add to the amount they could ask for its return. 'He's worth millions, so a good reward for its return won't hurt him.'

That was the wrong answer.

'A reward?' Black smiled at Fred. 'You want a reward?'

'Yeah, and a decent one.'

Black sighed. 'Okay. Mr Houseman, give the lad his reward please.'

Jerry Houseman moved towards Fred and shot him in the head, the noise reduced to a quiet '*phut*' by the silencer. Fred slumped sideways on the sofa, blood trickling down from the bullet hole in his forehead over his face into the sofa fabric.

Black turned to the other two boys. 'Anybody else like a reward?'

The shock had left the brothers speechless for a moment, before the gravity of their situation hit them.

'It's not here, we haven't got it here.' The panic in Harry's shaking voice showed through. The fear overwhelming George had rendered him totally speechless as Houseman's gun turned to point at his head.

'So where is it?' No more smiles as Black raised his gun to point it down at Harry.

'Sammy's got it.'

'Sammy? Do we have another member of this little gang?'

'Yes, Sammy.'

'Sammy who?'

'Sammy Johnson.'

'And where can I find this Sammy Johnson?'

'Along the landing, number eighty-six.'

'And you are sure I will find the laptop with Sammy? Absolutely sure?'

'Yes, yes, it's there. I swear it's there!'

'Good, I thought you'd see sense.' Black nodded to Houseman as he shot Harry in the head, and Houseman did the same to George.

They unscrewed the silencers from their guns and put them in their pockets, and the guns back into shoulder holsters under their coats

'At times like this I always try to think positively, Jerry,' said Black. 'One day in the future the situation might have been reversed, and one or all of those three could well have been standing over me with a gun. That won't happen now, will it?'

'Definitely won't happen now Trevor.' Jerry nodded as they left the flat, pulling the door shut after them, and they walked along the landing looking for number eighty-six.

'Give the magicians a call and have them clean the place up.'

'Okay.' Houseman took out his mobile and made the call as they walked along. The magicians, as they were known to those who used their bespoke services, were a pair of nameless individuals who made things disappear for money – quite a lot of money. The things they made disappear were usually bodies. They asked no questions and had no names; just an unregistered mobile number and an old Transit van carrying false plates.

****

Ten minutes earlier Sammy Johnson had been surprised to find the door to the Lanes' flat open. It was usually shut and bolted on the inside. Sammy was even more surprised to walk in to the hall and hear the conversation from the living room between the Lanes and Black about the laptop held under Sammy's arm. When two shots were fired in quick succession, Sammy thought it time to leave – to leave fast and get well away.

****

Trevor Black could put on an engaging smile when he had to. He rang the bell of number eighty-six and adopted his engaging smile when a late middle-aged lady opened the door. One look at her and he dropped the smile; he could see where she was coming from. Peroxide blonde with gray roots, scruffy black leather trousers with cigarette burns, fake Nike trainers and a Motörhead T-shirt faded by age and enhanced with spilled coffee stains. A cigarette hung from her lips and the overpowering smell

17

of stale cigarette smoke made its escape with the blast of warm air from within. Black looked at the peeling and torn wallpaper, the threadbare carpet, the solitary hanging lightbulb that had said goodbye to its shade long ago, and the broken child's bike leant against the wall. Money didn't live here.

He forced a smile back to his face. 'Hello, I'm sorry to trouble you, I wonder if I might have a word with Sammy?'

'Who are you, police?' asked the lady. 'You don't come in without a warrant.'

'The Lanes down the landing said Sammy may be able to help me find something.'

'Don't tell me, it's that fucking laptop I bet.'

'You've won your bet – now could I have a word with Sammy, please?' Black was beginning to get a bit annoyed.

'She's not here.'

That was a surprise. '*She*? Is Sammy a girl?'

'Last time I saw her she was – she's my daughter, Samantha. She went down to the Lanes' place ten minutes ago with the laptop – said it was worth a fortune. Surprised you didn't see her there.'

Black looked at Houseman. Had this girl been in the back of the Lanes' flat with the laptop all the time they were there? Maybe she'd come in halfway through and sussed what was happening and bolted. Maybe she'd heard or seen everything. If she had she wouldn't have hung about, and if she had Day's laptop they needed to find her.

Houseman moved back and looked down over the edge of the balcony wall. Six flights below Sammy was running across the parking area out of the estate. The street lights had come on as the evening drew in and the package clutched under her arm reflected their light and looked about the right size for a laptop.

****

DAY 2

'Who were they?' asked Palmer as he stepped over the crime scene tape and joined DS Gheeta Singh. They stood at the edge of an open grave in West London Cemetery, looking down at the bodies of three young men sprawled over one another where they had been dropped in. He'd been called at home as he got ready to go to the Yard that morning, as had his DS who had arrived at the scene thirty minutes before him. Singh's Barbican flat was nearer than his Dulwich Village house.

'No idea, guv, nothing to identify them.' Singh shook her head and turned up her coat collar to shield herself from the cold wind blowing across the cemetery as best she could. Each body had a single bullet hole in the forehead. Crime scene tape bordered a twenty-metre square around the open grave, taking in other adjacent 'occupied' graves and a mini-digger. The ground was being checked by local CSIs for footprints and plaster casts taken of any found. A police photographer took pictures of the bodies and the grave. Mourners passing by on their way to another burial rubber-necked from the footpath fifty meters away and asked each other, *what was going on*?

Singh continued, 'All three must have been dumped overnight. I've had a word with the gravedigger and he says this grave was dug late yesterday afternoon, ready for a funeral taking place this morning, and a tarpaulin cover put over it for the night in case it rained.'

'Bit of a surprise when he took off the tarpaulin this morning.'

'Be a bigger surprise if the tarpaulin had been left in place until the funeral party stood round the grave waiting to lower granddad into his last resting place guv.'

'Not the kind of place you'd expect to find squatters moved in overnight, eh?' Palmer smiled at his own remark.

DS Singh was used to Palmer's caustic remarks and ignored it. 'The Pathology van is on its way to take the bodies to the morgue for post mortems once Forensics have had a look.'

'Who's on forensics, Frome?'

'Yes.'

'Good.'

Reg Frome was Palmer's unofficial partner in crime solving. They both joined the Met as cadets at Henley College at the same time, and Palmer had progressed through the uniformed and then the detective ranks as Frome had progressed through the forensic science ranks. Frome was now head of Murder Forensics and was the 'go to' CSI for Palmer's Serial Murder Squad.

'Bit young, weren't they?' Palmer leant over the grave. 'Teenagers or early twenties I'd say.'

The uniformed OIC walked over. Gheeta introduced Palmer.

'DCS Palmer, nice to meet you. I'm Superintendent Hawkins, Hampstead CID.' Hawkins was just about regulation height and portly; probably spent too much time deskbound filling in Home Office reports, the scourge of senior officers in the force. 'I had the snapper send a picture across to my team room earlier and we've got a couple of leads on the deceased. Seems the three of them were known for petty theft, mainly breaking into cars in car parks and stealing dashcams and sat navs, that sort of thing. They are, or were, George and Harry Lane, and their cousin Frederick Smith. It's obviously a serial killing, not a crime we get a lot of in Hampstead, which is why my AC pushed it across to the Yard and your department. I'll do an official handover of the case to your office and send all the info we have on the deceased as soon as I get back.'

Palmer's eyes widened at the information. 'Good, that's good – very good. At least we have a starting point. I'd appreciate it if your men could do a sweep around the outside of the cemetery today before they leave, check the roads bordering it for shops or houses with CCTV and seize any taken in the last twenty-four hours. See if we can't pick up a suspicious vehicle, or maybe even the actual dumping of the bodies.'

He exchanged nods with Hawkins who happily left them to it. Filling in Home Office reports in a warm office was far more inviting than standing in a cold, windy cemetery.

A green Forensics van pulled up outside the cemetery gates and Reg Frome got out from the passenger door, already clothed in his green plastic suit and over shoes, he was followed by four CSI officers similarly dressed from the back doors. He made his way into the cemetery, meeting the local chief CSI officer and exchanging a few words as he was brought up to speed, before making his way over to Palmer and Singh. Without his CSI hairnet holding his hair in check, Frome resembled 'Doc' Brown from the film *Back to The Future*, with a shock of brilliant white hair that seemed uncontrollable.

He gave them a nod. 'Morning, Justin – morning, Sergeant.' They returned his greeting as he looked into the grave. 'Not the kind of funeral their parents would have wished for, is it?'

Palmer was getting colder by the minute, and as a sun-lover the onset of the British late autumn with winter to follow wasn't very appealing, and the allure of his warm Team Room at the Yard and a hot coffee was getting stronger by the second. 'We've got a lead from the local boys as to who they are Reg, but confirmation by prints and DNA would help. Can't do much without that, just in case we get it wrong – don't want to send FLOs to the wrong parents.'

Frome understood and nodded. 'Local CSI officer says they've finished doing the ground work around the grave, so let's get the bodies out and take a look.'

He beckoned three of his plastic-suited forensic officers and had two drop into the grave and pass up the bodies, which the third laid on open body bags. Frome patted them down and checked the pockets.

'Nothing here, Justin – empty pockets. I'll get the prints and DNA swabs done and see if we can't come up with confirmation of the names off the databases back at the office and fast track them over to you.' The black Pathology Transit pulled up outside. Frome noticed it. 'The Path lab's here, they'll get a time of death from the post mortems. I don't think it's too long ago – still a bit of colour in the skin and full rigor mortis hasn't set in yet. But that's their job, not mine.'

'Right.' Palmer blew warmth into his cupped hands and rubbed them together. 'Nothing more we can do here, Sergeant.' He pulled his overcoat lapels up further to shield against the wind. 'May as well go to the office and wait for things to happen.'

'I'll catch you up there, guv,' Gheeta said. 'I want to find the gravedigger and have another word, try and jog his memory. He was the first one in early this morning and made the 999 call, so maybe he noticed something out of the ordinary.'

'Like three bodies appearing overnight in his grave.' Palmer smiled. 'He's probably been sedated.'

****

Nothing noteworthy happened during the rest of the day. Forensics and autopsy reports would be ready the next day, so Claire, the civilian office clerk who worked back in the Team Room on the second floor of the Yard, started pulling together as much information on the deceased as she could from various databases, both crime-related and educational. Claire holds the fort when the team are out and uses her computer skills to back up Gheeta with in-depth searching of social media and websites related to names or places in a case, hunting for hidden clues and threads that can break it open. Gheeta had persuaded Palmer to have Claire transferred from the Yard's IT department to help her in the basic detection work, as more and more of it shifted from physical clues to cyber, social media, mobile phone and CCTV analysis in the ever growing digital world that criminals took advantage of. The other side of the coin is the major advantage the digital world gives to crime-solving, in the fact that once information is on a computer or mobile phone it can never be deleted. Your computer hard drive holds your life story, forever.

Palmer sat in his office across the corridor from the Team Room, heater full on, reading through the files on the deceased that

26

Hawkins had emailed through from Hampstead and that Claire had printed off. As Hawkins had said, three petty thieves was about the mark of the deceased; so why should somebody need to have three petty thieves killed, and killed professionally at that? What had these three kids stumbled on that signed their death warrants?

When Gheeta returned to the Team Room she gave the white progress board that was fixed on the far end wall a good clean and wrote up the three boys' names; Claire would unearth pictures from the boys' files that would be pinned up later. The basics were being laid out, as with every case; all that was needed now was a lead to follow. A thread joining the deceased to their killer or killers, a thread that would point Palmer in the right direction. It was there somewhere, it always was, they just needed to find it.

****

'Three bodies in an open grave? That's awful.'

Having been married to Palmer for fifty-plus years, not a lot shocked Mrs P.; but three young bodies dumped in an open grave had come close.

'Yes, not a pretty sight.' Palmer had been dropped off at his house in Dulwich Village at the end of the day by a patrol car. Sometimes he'd take his own Honda CRV to the Yard – he had a marked parking place – but that day he'd not felt like entering the stressful world of London commuter traffic and had called for a car to take him to the cemetery when he'd got the call at breakfast time earlier that day. And why not? His pay grade sanctioned the use of a driven car, and he very rarely took one.

He was sat on the bottom stair in the hall and taking off his shoes as Daisy, his eleven year-old Springer gave him a welcoming nudge and got a pat and a hug in return, before taking one of his slippers in her mouth, walking up the hall back to the front door and dropping it.

'Oi! Bring that back. Daisy, bring it back.'

Nah, thought Daisy, can't be bothered, and sauntered back past him towards the kitchen, from where the aroma of toad-in-the-hole coming from the oven was infinitely more inviting than Palmer's old slipper.

Palmer fetched the slipper and followed the dog into the kitchen, where Mrs P., wearing oven gloves, was taking the toad-in-the-hole from the oven and putting it on the laid table.

'That looks good.' Palmer took a portion onto his plate from the serving dish, a big portion. Toad-in-the-hole was one of his favourite meals. 'I hope these are beef sausages and not veggie.'

In Mrs P.'s ongoing life's work of trying to wean Palmer onto healthier food, she had occasionally slipped a veggie sausage or a tofu or soya-based meat product onto his plate. Sometimes she won, sometimes she didn't.

'No, they're beef from the local butchers.' She sat down to her own plate and looked at the depleted serving dish. 'Oh, nice of you to leave me a portion, Justin,' she said sarcastically. 'It was three sausages each, not four for you and two for me.'

Palmer didn't reply; sometimes he'd found it best not to.

'Who were these three lads?' Mrs P. asked, serving herself.

'Well,' Palmer answered between mouthfuls, 'We know their names – seems like two brothers and a cousin, all with minor records and a pretty poor upbringing in care homes and detention centres, but that's about it. Petty thieves, breaking into cars and sheds, that sort of thing. Nothing major.'

'Oh, that reminds me – Benji has a new garden shed. Did you notice it on your way in?'

'No. He's already got a garden shed, why get another one?'

Benji, full name Benjamin Courtney-Smythe, was Palmer's next-door neighbour and nemesis. A rather portly retired advertising executive in his early sixties, with spray-on tan, a ponytail pulled together from his receding hairline, designer clothes, and, in Palmer's estimation, of questionable sexual orientation judging by the mincing walk and habit of waving a floppy hand about when talking. Not that that worried Palmer, who didn't have a problem with Pride – although transgender baffled him a bit. Too much money and too much time on his hands was Palmer's usual anti-Benji mantra; three or four continental cruises or holidays and a new motor every year, and Palmer reckoned a new nip and tuck every year too.

But Benji was a great favourite with most of the ladies in the area, especially Mrs P. and her gardening club and WI; this rankled a bit with Palmer, who used to be their favourite until

Benji moved in and knocked him off that plinth. Then, to cap it all, Benji ran for the local council elections and got voted in; he was soon elevated to Council Chairperson and became everybody's favourite by reinstating free bus passes for pensioners and free pool passes for the over 50's. He then topped it off by twisting arms at the county level to secure funding to re-open the library that the previous council had closed due to financial cuts. But he was also prone to accidents, usually involving Palmer's property or person.

'What does he need another garden shed for? These sausages are tasty.'

'Mining.'

'Mining, in a shed? What's he going to do, start digging for gold on the quiet?'

'No, he's going to mine Bitcoin. You know what that is, don't you?'

'Yes, the latest way for criminals to launder money, that's what that is – crypto-currency.'

'Correct – my-oh-my, Justin, you are up to date,' Mrs P. added feigning surprise, but also slightly impressed. 'Apparently you *'mine'* it by running computer programmes that build the coins with a *consensus mechanism that forms a blockchain of nodes*, Benji told me that

31

and I have no idea what it means, except that he is installing a hundred computers in that shed to start the mining and it takes tons of electricity and computer time.'

'He'll get a knock on the door from the Narcotics Squad.'

'Why, it's not illegal, is it? No drugs involved.'

'No, but the computers will generate enough heat that the shed roof will show up on the heat sensor cameras the Drug Squad use attached to drones or helicopters to pinpoint marijuana being grown in houses and warehouses. Those plants have to be kept hot and the heat rises and shows up on the sensors. Three marijuana busts down the road in Peckham recently have turned out to be banks of computers mining crypto-currency giving off the heat, and not marijuana plants at all. The crooks bypass the electricity metres onto the main grid – normal residential electrical consumption wouldn't do the job, nowhere near powerful enough. Benji's going to love his next electric bill! He'll need the first bitcoin he mines to pay it!'

****

DAY 3

Trevor Black dried himself after a long morning shower and put on fresh clothes. The old ones went into a bin bag destined for the local tip, even if they were an expensive silk cloth suit. He had a habit of destroying clothes that he'd worn at a 'job'. Forensics were too good these days, and he didn't take chances. His mobile buzzed. He picked it up and answered.

'Yes?'

It was Robert Day, a nasty individual who had spent his life making other people's lives miserable. Day had come to the UK from China as an illegal in the nineties and started people trafficking whilst all the other lowlifes in London were still pushing drugs on street corners. The people he brought in were Asians or from the Middle East, whose families paid a fortune for a new life in Britain for their children, only to find that when they arrive their new life was tending marijuana plants in converted warehouses or working in Day's takeaways or Indian and Chinese restaurants; or, if female, forced into sex work. Day houses them in overcrowded cheap back street houses at exorbitant rents that they never earn enough to pay off, and so they build up a debt with him that ties them to him for ever, or until more money from the family back home is sent to pay the debt off and release them. If they walk away before the debt is paid, his *people* find them and they disappear – Black and Houseman being his *people*. You couldn't mistake his clipped Chinese way of speaking English.

'You get it?'

'No, it wasn't there.'

'They tell you where it is?'

'Yes, there's a fourth member of the team – Samantha Johnson. Ever heard of her?'

'No, where she then?

'Don't know, she did a runner.'

'Them others will know where she gone. Give them slap.'

'Too late.'

'Why it too late?'

'They're dead and buried.'

'You kid me?'

'No, you pay me to do a job and I'll do it. Don't panic, you'll get the laptop back.'

'You make sure I do. I want laptop, Trevor. That what I paying you for, not to knock off kids.'

'I know, and I'll find it. We know this girl has got it so we've just got to find her. Relax, I know what I'm doing.'

The phone clicked off. Black speed-dialled another number.

Houseman answered. 'Yeah?'

'You on your way?'

'Yeah. I'll be outside in five.'

'Okay, I'll come down.'

Black checked himself in the wall mirror. Smart in a fawn suit, with brown brogues, black hair smoothed back, moustache trimmed and tie knotted, he looked every inch a businessman not every inch a nasty bastard enforcer who did the deeds that his criminal friends wanted done without any fuss, and without any repercussions landing their way. But Trevor Black had made a mistake this time – a big mistake: Samantha Johnson.

****

Palmer entered the Team Room, taking off his coat and draping it over a table. 'Morning, Claire. Anything happening yet?'

Gheeta had already phoned Claire and told her to expect some files from Hawkins at Hampstead, and that she was going to the cemetery for another word with the gravedigger on her way in.

'Couple of files come over from Hampstead, sir – I've printed them out. Sergeant Singh is going to stop by the cemetery and have another chat with the gravedigger on her way in.' She pointed to the papers lying on a trestle table. Palmer pulled up a government issue metal chair and sat down to read them. Each of the dead boys was known for petty theft; their *modus operandi* was to select a car with a sat nav, dash cam, computer or mobile phone, or anything of value the owner had left visible that was easy to sell on, they would break a window, take the goods and split, leaving the crime scene in different directions to confuse any witnesses. The goods were quickly pawned under false names to dodgy pawn shops who knew the lads and knew they'd not come back to redeem them, so they would put them on sale straight away, or they sold them on eBay. Any recovered were always free of prints, and that type of petty crime didn't warrant a lot of serious police time. 'If you leave a computer in full view on a car seat then what do you expect?' would be the regular police answer to your report of the theft, 'Claim on your insurance.' So this little trio of thieves had enjoyed a pretty easy life of petty crime, until… Until what?

Palmer sat back when he finished reading the files. What had they done that got them killed, and professionally killed at that with a single bullet to the head? His thoughts were interrupted by Gheeta's arrival. She slung her coat on the table next to his and settled her backside on a radiator.

'More like mid-winter out there today, not autumn.'

'The files on the deceased are through.' Palmer pointed to the papers on the table.

Gheeta nodded as she rubbed her hands together. 'Yes, read them in the squad car on the way here, guv. Interesting, eh?'

Palmer was confused. 'How did you get them in the squad car?'

'On my phone, guv.' She pulled her iPhone from her trouser pocket. 'Technology, guv – Claire sent them to me by email.'

Palmer nodded as though he understood. He did just about, but technology wasn't his strong point, which was why he'd insisted on Gheeta joining him from the yard's Cyber unit; he readily admitted that had been the best move he'd ever made in his long career. Her continual updating of his squad's hard- and software with files, apps and programmes both legal and, ahem, not always *totally* legal, had kept him abreast and sometimes ahead in the war against ever more sophisticated serial killers. Mrs P. had said it was the best thing he'd done in years, as '*you can't teach an old dog new tricks, Justin*' – not that he appreciated being called an *old dog*. Eleven year-old Daisy was an *old dog*, but it was true, you can't teach an old dog new tricks, as shown when he had tried to get Daisy to sit up and beg, and she'd just laid down and given him a look that said, '*no chance*'.

'Interesting chat with the gravedigger, guv,' Gheeta carried on. 'Nothing caught his attention yesterday until he lifted the tarpaulin and saw the bodies, but this morning, with his mind settled down after the shock had worn off, he noticed something else – *two* piles of earth beside the grave.'

'Two?' Palmer couldn't see the significance.

'Yes, usually a couple of them of them dig the graves using that small JCB digger the night before any funerals are due, and the soil they remove is put in a neat pile a little way away from the grave and replaced to cover the coffin after the funeral when the mourners have left. But, and it's a big but, there's only ever *one* pile.'

'So where did the second pile come from?'

'Exactly. He took me over to the grave and he thinks somebody dug out more earth because the hole is now too deep for a coffin to be lowered all the way into it. The lowering straps wouldn't be long enough so more earth has been dug out, and he reckons that's the second pile.'

Palmer was getting the picture. 'So whoever brought the bodies probably intended digging the grave deeper, putting the bodies in and then covering them with the soil, bringing the grave floor back up to normal depth?'

'Yes, and then the funeral goes ahead with the coffin being interned above the bodies and the grave filled back in, and nobody is any the wiser that it has four bodies in it and not just one. Brilliant.'

'So why didn't it happen?'

'He reckons whoever it was had planned to use the digger but couldn't because it had a flat battery, That's why he came in early yesterday morning – he'd had it on charge at home overnight and was going to put it back in the digger and finish the job, plus he'd another grave to dig for the afternoon. He says two spades are missing from his shed. No sign of them, but whoever brought the bodies to the cemetery must have been going to use the digger, but when they couldn't, they dug as much as they could with the spades, but time beat them.'

'Or they were disturbed whilst digging it.'

'Could have been when he came in early with the battery to finish the job and get the other grave dug.'

'And so the burial party just chucked the bodies in the open grave, put the tarpaulin back and fled.'

'No other answer is there, guv?'

'None I can think of at the moment. But that does pose a big question, doesn't it – how many other two-tier graves are there around?'

'Others?' Claire asked turning from her keyboard.

'Yes, stands to reason, doesn't it? Let's face it, it's a brilliant way to get rid of a body – bury it under another legally buried one.'

'You think it's been done before?' Gheeta raised her eyebrows.

'Definitely, it's not something you'd think of on the spur of the moment, is it? This is a planned pro job. I wouldn't mind betting there's a few other two-tier graves in that cemetery. It's perfect – graves dug the night before a funeral and a digger on site, easy and foolproof. Once the funeral is over, how can you tell if the grave has an extra stiff down below? You can't. Put a cadaver dog in and it's going to point at every grave isn't it, because there's at least one body in each. The dog can't tell whether it's one or two, and to find out you'd need to exhume all the graves – at least all those from the last decade. I can't see Bateman sanctioning that on his budget.'

Assistant Commissioner Bateman, Palmer's immediate superior, was forty-eight years old, slightly built and the epitome of a social climber in society, but the ladder he was intent on climbing was in the police force; he sucked up to anybody in authority that he thought might assist in his self planned career path towards his ultimate goal of being Commissioner. He was always immaculately turned out in a uniform with ironed creases so sharp they could cut bread.

His nemesis was his head, in that it was bald, totally bald. It didn't worry anybody except AC Bateman, who had tried every remedy advertised to re-thatch his dome: potions, creams, massages and all sorts of oils had failed to deliver on their promised results. It was hereditary; his father had been bald, his brother was bald, and he wasn't sure but he had a suspicion that his elder sister had started to weave false hairpieces into her receding locks at an early age. He had once tried wearing a wig, but the silence from everybody in the Yard on the day he wore it, and the number of officers who kept their hand in front of their faces to cover broad smiles as he walked past put paid to that idea.

There had always been a distrustful undercurrent to Palmer and Bateman's relationship; nothing you could pin down, but Palmer didn't like or agree with fast-tracking of university graduates to management positions in the force. He'd have them do the two years on the beat first; see how they handled a seventeen stone drug dealer waving a ten-inch knife, intent on avoiding arrest at all costs. Bateman, on the other hand, would like to be surrounded with graduates with '*firsts*' in various '*ologies*' and was very pleased when the Government brought in the minimum recruitment requirement of having to have a degree in order to even apply to join the force. He believed the old school coppers like Palmer were outdated dinosaurs, and that crime could be solved by elimination and computer programmes, which is why he had tried unsuccessfully to transfer DS Singh away from Palmer and back into the Cyber Crime Unit from where Palmer had originally poached her. Bateman had no time for an experienced detective's accumulated knowledge being an asset in the war against crime, and the sooner he could shut down the Serial Murder Squad and combine it with the Organised Crime Unit, CID and Cyber Crime the better. Cutting costs was paramount in Bateman's personal mission statement.

The trouble was that Palmer's team, the Organised Crime Unit, CID and Cyber Crime were producing good case solved figures which the political masters at the Home Office liked, and they therefore insisted the units carried on working as they were, and Bateman had to shelve his combination scheme for the time being. But what really irked Bateman most was that they really liked Palmer too. The press also liked Palmer, and the rank and file loved him.

Gheeta agreed with Palmer. No way would Bateman let his budget be used to dig out other graves on the off-chance of some being two-tier. 'And what about other cemeteries?' she asked. 'If they've got a digger, which I would think they all have these days, any of them could have double graves as well.'

Palmer nodded. 'I think it best we just stick to the current case, eh? I'll make a report on our suspicions that this method could have been used before and pass it to Cold Case Unit – that will cover our backs.'

Both Gheeta and Claire nodded. The internal phone rang and Claire answered it.

'SMS.'

Palmer looked at Gheeta and mouthed the question, 'SMS?'

'Serial Murder Squad, guv – you remember? The squad you're in charge of. They use this room?' She swept a hand round indicating the room.

Palmer knew when he was being wound up. 'All right, all right, just I hadn't heard her use the initials before.'

Claire covered the mouthpiece with her hand. 'There's a Henry Gooch in reception who would like a word, sir. Apparently he's the Lanes' probation officer.'

Gheeta and Palmer raised their eyebrows to each other.

'This could be interesting.' Palmer nodded to Claire. 'Go and bring him up if you would, Claire.'

****
**

Henry Gooch was late middle-aged, carrying too much weight from a career spent sitting at a desk; third generation Afro-English in a rumpled dark suit and equally rumpled shirt, with short, neat dreadlocks hanging on his forehead. He carried a document file under one arm. The introductions over, Palmer indicated a table and took a seat with Gooch and Gheeta.

'Well then.' Palmer gave Gooch one of his smiles. 'What can you tell us, Mr Gooch?'

'Henry, just Henry, please.' Gooch smiled back. 'It's about the Lanes – Superintendent Hawkins at Hampstead told me to contact you. I am, or I was, the Lanes' probation officer. I've got all their records, criminal and otherwise, and maybe there's something in them that can lead you to the killer? They weren't bad lads, Superintendent.'

'Chief Superintendent.' Palmer pulled up Gooch on his rank, just as Gheeta knew he would; just as he did when anybody didn't use the full title. '*It's taken me forty odd years to get that rank, and so people can damn well use it,*' was his reply when Gheeta pulled him up explaining civilians wouldn't know the difference between a Superintendent and a Chief Superintendent.

Palmer softened his rebuke at Gooch with a smile. 'So they weren't bad kids then, eh?' He looked at the papers Claire had given him that Hawkins had emailed over. 'George Lane – twelve convictions for theft, breaking and entering, and car theft, total four years in a young offender's institute. Harry Lane – seven convictions and five years in a young offender's institute. Frederick Smith – seven convictions and four years inside.' He looked up at Gooch. 'I wonder if all those people they stole from, all the people whose homes they broke into or all the people who lost their belongings and never got them back would agree with you that they *weren't bad lads?*'

Gooch shrugged. 'Chief Superintendent…' He was struggling to explain. 'What I mean is yes, of course they were bad in that way, but they were never violent – and compared with the majority of young men that I have to try and put back onto the straight and narrow, they really weren't bad. No drug dealing – stopped and searched many times and never carrying weapons.'

'Family?' Palmer expected to find the boys came from a family of criminals.

'Broken family.' Gooch shrugged. 'Same goes for most of my young clients. Parents weren't married, split up when George was three and Harry two, so from then on they were in care, being shunted around different homes and carers until George was sixteen and was put into a council flat, where Harry joined him a year later. Frederick is their cousin and suffered the same fate, although his was a single mother – the sister of George and Harry's mother. She had him at sixteen and so he went into care as well. Same age as George.'

Palmer was more interested in the mention of a flat than the sob story. 'This council flat they were put in, is that where they were living now?'

'Yes.'

'Does Superintendent Hawkins know where it is?'

'Yes, of course.'

Palmer looked at Gheeta; both were surprised that Hawkins hadn't mentioned it. 'Give Hawkins a ring, Sergeant. Get that flat sealed off and then give Reg Frome a bell and have him take a look.'

Gheeta nodded and left the table to make the calls. Palmer turned back to Gooch. 'So, why are three lads who rank as small time petty thieves subject of what seems to be, at first glance, a professional hit?'

Gooch shrugged and took a deep breath. 'I have no idea, that's why I brought their records with me. You may find something in there of interest, but I just can't make head nor tail of it.' He took the document file and put it on the table. 'Keep this as long as you like – copies of the boys' probation files, social and psychiatric reports, that sort of thing. May be something in there.'

'Did they work alone?'

'What do you mean?'

'Were they part of a bigger gang? They've upset somebody big time, the question is who and how?'

'No, no, as far as I know they kept themselves to themselves. You need to talk to Sammy, she'd know more than me.'

'Sammy?'

'Samantha, Samantha Johnson, George's girlfriend – she lives with her mother a few doors away on the same landing in the block of flats, number 86. I don't think they had anything serious going on but she'd sometimes come with him when he and I had meetings and wait in reception for him. Nice girl. I had hoped they might settle down somewhere together and he'd sort himself out. That's not going to happen now.'

'No, it's not.' Palmer stood up. 'Well thank you for coming, Henry, very much appreciated – I'll get these records back to you as soon as we've had a good look. If you think of anything else that might be of help, please let me know.'

Gooch took the hint and they shook hands. He gave Gheeta, who was still on the phone, a wave and Claire escorted him out and down the stairs to the foyer.

Gheeta came off the phone as Claire returned. Palmer sat back down, took a deep breath and stretched his arms above his head as Gheeta sat down opposite.

'Hawkins thought you knew about the flat. He's sealing it now. I told him our Forensics were going in. Mr Frome says he can get over this afternoon. He reckons to have the ballistics report on the bullets by then too.'

'Good. What do you make of Gooch?'

'I wouldn't have his job for all the tea in China.'

'I've never thought probation works with these young criminals.'

Palmer stood and wandered over to look out of the picture window across the embankment to the Thames. 'They quickly learn to play the system – benefit payments, free council flats, and all the do-gooders saying it's not their fault they mug old ladies, it's the fault of society. They twist people like Gooch round their little fingers.'

'Bring back the birch then, guv?' Gheeta gave a wry smile to Claire.

Palmer turned and put on a false air of being offended. 'Good heavens no, Sergeant – no need to go that far. The stocks would be quite sufficient.'

****

'I hope you're fucking joking?'

Trevor Black was sitting in the driver's seat of his Lexus in the underground residents' car park of his apartment block in Nine Elms, Wandsworth. It was called an executive apartment block and had risen from the demolished area of Victorian warehouses that once fronted the Thames wharfs along the south side of the river. The whole area was now a row of bland high rise executive apartment blocks with *river views* and exorbitant service charges that people like Trevor Black could afford. He looked across at Jerry Houseman who had parked his car and joined him in the Lexus.

Houseman shook his head. 'No, I'm not.'

'I paid them five grand to do that job – fucking twats. What went wrong?'

'The digger wouldn't start.'

'Wouldn't start? What do you mean, wouldn't start?'

'No battery, the battery had been taken out.'

'Jesus Christ. So what did they do, just leave the bodies there?'

'They dug as much as they could with a couple of spades they found in a shed. Not enough time, though – they had to scarper when the gravedigger turned up.'

'I want that five grand back, and then I'm going to show them what happens if you cross Trevor Black.'

'Calm down, Trevor, nobody can connect the bodies to us. The police will just put it down to another local postcode drugs war.'

'You been past there today?'

'Yeah, I took a look on my way here. Coppers everywhere, got the place taped off.'

'Right, let's find this Sammy girl and get Day's laptop back before the police start poking around.'

'Where do we start?'

'Back at that shitty Bevan estate. She must have some friends there, and they'll know where she hangs out.'

****

In the Team Room Palmer slung the Lanes' probation records onto the desk in front of him and rubbed his eyes.

'Not a lot of interest in there. Give Hawkins another ring, Sergeant – apologise for being a pain and see if he can give us a list of the Lanes' victims, people and places they stole from. Might give us a lead – they obviously hit on somebody they shouldn't have, somebody who was upset enough to take the ultimate revenge. Then I think we'll take a trip to the lads' flat and see if Reg Frome has found anything, and whilst we are there pop along and have a chat with this Sammy girl.'

****

'Not much space, is there? Could do with a coat of paint too.'

Palmer stood in the living room at the Lanes' flat wearing a white CSI paper over-suit, plastic gloves, elasticated hairnet and over-shoes. The place was jammed with Frome's CSI team working their way centimetre by centimetre through the rooms.

'Two bedrooms, a living room and a kitchen, guv – what more could you want?' Gheeta came out of the bedroom dressed the same, followed by Reg Frome and a snapper.

'I've seen worse,' Frome added. 'And so have you, Justin.'

Palmer nodded. 'True. Right then, what have we got?'

Frome shrugged. 'Not much, I'm afraid. The whole place has been cleaned – professional job, bleach sprayed on everything so no prints and no DNA. We found some blood in the sofa material, I'll get that grouped but no doubt it will be the same group as the Lanes' – we'll get that from the path report. I'm having the digger at the cemetery dusted for prints, but if it was the same people who did the cleaning job here I'm not hopeful.'

Palmer pursed his lips as he thought hard. 'Why? Why would somebody go to the trouble and expense of having a magician come in and clean up? Why?'

'A magician?' The snapper stopped taking pictures of the room and turned to Palmer. 'What's a magician got to do with it?'

'It's slang, son – like *snapper* meaning photographer. A magician in criminal circles is a person or persons who make things disappear, like evidence and bodies. If you ever think about a career change I understand it's very well-paid.' He gave the snapper a smile.

Gheeta's laptop pinged in its shoulder bag. She took it out and opened it.

'Ballistics report is in, guv.' She read and scrolled. 'Two different guns used, two different 9mm bullets taken from the deceased. Both guns are known and on file and both have been used before in similar circumstances – those similar circumstances being bodies shot in the head. Eight to date, guv – six with one gun, two with the other.'

Frome looked at Palmer. 'Hitmen. How are these lads so dangerous that somebody hires a pair of pros to silence them?'

Palmer shrugged. 'You tell me. Let's hope this Sammy girl can throw some light on it.'

'Sammy?' Frome asked.

'Apparently George Lane had a girlfriend, Samantha Johnson – known as Sammy, lives a few doors along. We are going to have a word with her before we leave. How long will you be here for?'

'Oh, ages yet – 'til early evening at least.'

'Okay, we'll pop in after seeing the girl just in case anything turns up.'

****

'She's not here.'

'Who's not here?' Palmer took a small step back from the doorway as Motörhead T-shirt thrust herself forward in a threatening manner. He had hardly taken his finger off the broken doorbell and rattled the letter box before Motörhead had opened the door and snarled her greeting.

'Samantha, she's not here. I told your mates that yesterday, she's not been back since. Now piss off before I call the police.'

Palmer pointed a finger in the direction of Sergeant Singh in full uniform, standing a couple of metres along the walkway. 'The police are already here, madam.' He pulled his warrant card from his inside pocket and opened it, holding it up to Motörhead's face. 'You want to talk to me here or at the police station?'

Motörhead backed off a step and folded her arms. 'It's terrible, them boys being murdered like that – gives the neighbourhood a bad name. We might not all be angels round here, but nobody deserves that. What did they do?'

Palmer thought about asking to go inside to talk, but decided against it as the all-pervading smell of cigarette smoke coming from inside wasn't something he wanted to take home on his clothes. 'We don't know what they did, Mrs...?'

'Johnson, I'm Samantha's mother. I suppose you want to talk to her like your mates did?'

'Our mates?'

'Them two officers what came round yesterday asking questions, I told them everything I know so I've nothing to add.'

'I think you'd better describe the two officers Mrs Johnson because as far as I am aware no officers have been here, whoever they were they weren't police officers, so if they come back I suggest you ask for their warrant cards and give us a call'

Gheeta stepped forward taking her laptop from its shoulder bag, 'Can you describe them Mrs Johnson?'

She did, as best she could as Gheeta tapped her descriptions into her laptop.

'What are you after Samantha for anyway? What's she done?'

'Maybe nothing Mrs Johnson,' Palmer smiled.

'So why are you here?'

' Mr Gooch told us she was George's girlfriend. She might be able to throw some light on who would want to kill them.'

'Who's Mr Gooch?'

'Probation officer.'

'Samantha's not on probation.'

'George Lane was, apparently – she'd go with him to his meetings with his probation officer.'

Motörhead shook her head. 'Don't know nothing about that. She keeps herself to herself does Sammy. Best thing to do round here – what you don't know can't hurt you.'

'Who'd want to hurt the Lanes?'

'Don't know, but I'll put money on that fucking laptop having something to do with it.'

'What laptop?'

'The one them two blokes were after yesterday. Samantha said it was George's and worth a load of money. She had it with her last time I saw her.'

'Which was?'

'Yesterday, just before them two called here. Haven't seen her since.'

'Any idea where she might be?'

'Not really, sometimes I don't see her from one week to the next. She could be at Cathy's, her sister's place.'

'Where is her sister's place?'

'Peabody block, number eight. Turn left out of this block and it's the one behind us.'

'Do you have a picture of your daughter?' asked Gheeta.

'Cath or Sammy?'

'Sammy.'

'Hang on.' Motörhead disappeared inside and returned with a framed photo of Samantha Johnson taken at her last year at school. 'Taken five years ago. Did well at school, she did – could have made something of her life, then fell in with that Lane lot. I did warn her, but kids don't take any notice, do they?' She passed the picture to Gheeta.

'May I take a copy?' Gheeta asked.

'Yeah, why not? Her hair's short now.' Motörhead pointed to the girl's long hair. 'Lovely it was then, but she had it cut – said it got in the way. God knows in the way of what, but there you are, you can't argue with her. Changes colour all the time too – I never know what colour it's going to be when she walks in. Bloody bright green last time.'

Gheeta took a photo with her iPhone and passed the picture back. 'Thank you.'

Palmer pulled a contact card from his pocket and passed it over. 'If Samantha comes here would you ask her to give us a call please, Mrs Johnson? She could be in danger.'

Motörhead read the card. 'Detective Chief Superintendent, eh? My ex used to say any copper above a sergeant sat at a desk pushing paperclips around and drinking tea all day.' She laughed.

Gheeta smiled.

Palmer didn't. 'Your ex was wrong, Mrs Johnson – and anyway, I prefer coffee. Thanks for your time.' He turned to walk away and stopped, as though remembering something, and turned back to Motörhead. 'One more thing: the pair that visited you yesterday. Whoever they were, they weren't police officers, so if they come back I suggest you ask for their warrant cards and give us a call.' He gave Motörhead a brisk nod and walked away, followed by Gheeta, as Motörhead disappeared inside with a worried look on her face and closed her door, slipping the security chain across.

'Just a minute, guv.' Gheeta stopped and Palmer turned back towards her. 'I just want to have a chat to number 92.' She pointed to the door of number 92 which was facing down the walkway from a corner position further along.

Palmer waited as Gheeta went to 92 and pressed the bell. He knew better than to ask her what she was doing as his experience working with her for a few years told him that whatever she was doing at number 92 would be of benefit to the case. An older lady answered the door and glanced at Gheeta's warrant card; they talked for a couple of minutes and then she went back inside, leaving the door open. Gheeta signalled Palmer to wait. Knowing his sergeant as he did, Palmer was in no hurry. The lady came back to the door and passed Gheeta a piece of paper. Gheeta gave the lady her contact card and passed pleasantries before the lady went back inside and shut the door, Gheeta rejoined Palmer.

'Bingo!' Gheeta had a big smile.

'You look like the cat who got the cream, Sergeant.'

'I'm the sergeant who got the wi-fi doorbell, guv.'

Palmer was not a techie person; after all, that's why he had Gheeta transferred to his squad. He spread his hands. 'Explain.'

'It's one of those nerdy technical things that I know you just love, guv. I was looking around hoping to find a CCTV camera on the landing so we could back track on it and maybe find out who the two chaps that called at Mrs Johnson's yesterday were, as they were most probably the hitmen, right?'

'Could be, yes.'

'Well, I noticed 92 has a wi-fi video doorbell. You know what that is, guv?'

'Yes, seen them advertised on the TV.'

'Right, well the one at 92 sends a signal to her son's iPhone continuously, and if somebody presses the bell it alerts him so he can talk to them and see them via the phone. Anybody thinking it's just an old lady at home then thinks he's inside as well – it's a bit of security for his mum. But the bottom line is, it's on all of the time recording, so unless he deletes every day he should have images of the two men at number 78 and number 86. I've left my number with his mum and asked that he calls me when he gets home from work – then I'll get him to download yesterday's file to us and we can take a look at them.'

'Let's hope he hasn't deleted them.' Palmer could have praised Gheeta for noticing the bell, but he didn't. Palmer very, very rarely praised anybody; after all, it was their job to notice things. 'Right then, next stop number 8 Peabody.'

Palmer poked his head in at the Lanes' flat on their way past to see if Frome's team had found anything significant. They hadn't, so he and Gheeta made their way down the stairs to Peabody Block.

At the bottom of the stairs they turned left as Motörhead had told them to and then rounded the corner of the block, out of sight of

Trevor Black and Jerry Houseman coming round from the other end.

'She should never have got involved with the Lanes – I told her they were trouble, you can tell. No jobs and always had plenty of money – I've been on the benefits myself, and I know you don't get that sort of money. Sammy swore they weren't dealing, but I had my doubts.'

Samantha Johnson's sister Cathy was obviously her elder sister. She was early thirties, neatly dressed in jeans and blouse with shoulder length well-groomed hair. The flat was neat and tidy, minimalistic in furniture and ornaments. Palmer's warrant card had gained him and Gheeta entry. People on inner London estates like the Bevan don't want neighbours to see them talking to the police; neighbours might jump to the wrong conclusions.

'She's not staying with you then?' Gheeta asked.

'No, she popped in yesterday and told me about the shootings, but she didn't stay. Probably didn't fancy sleeping on the sofa – it's only two bedrooms and I've two young sons, so one for me and one for them. I'm on the housing list for a three bed, but they're gold dust round here. Which reminds me…' She checked her watch. 'I have to pick them up from school in forty minutes. Single mum, chucked the old man out two years ago – waste of time, he was. Married seven years and he spent six of them inside.'

'We won't keep you long. Tell me, did your sister leave anything here?' Palmer hoped against hope that Sammy had left the laptop that everybody seemed so interested in.

'No, I thought she was going back to mum's. Didn't she?'

'No, your mother thought she might have stayed here for the night.'

'No, she didn't. She was a bit shook up over the shooting – bit angry too.'

'Angry?' Palmer raised his eyebrows.

'Yes, said she knew who did it.'

'Who?'

'No idea, she didn't say and I didn't ask. Best to stay well away from that sort of thing round here – walls have ears. Keep yourself to yourself and mind your own business.'

'Did she have a laptop with her?' Gheeta asked.

'Yes, pretty old one – said she was going to sell it, said it was very valuable. Must have been a rare one 'cause you can get them for twenty quid at the Sunday boot. She liked all that techie stuff – everybody round here knows that if their computer packs up or gets a virus, Sammy can fix it for a few quid. I gave her a Tesco bag to put it in. You can't wander round here with a laptop on show or sooner or later a moped will pull up beside you and the bloke on the back will snatch it. Daren't even make a mobile phone call without checking around first. You want to get some of your uniforms round here now and again – never see any, we don't.'

Palmer didn't want to get into that old chestnut. 'Does she have a regular buyer for that sort of stuff?'

'No, most people tell her what they want and she comes up with it for them. I think she had a buyer for that one though 'cause she was fiddling with it on the kitchen table, had the back off.'

Palmer nodded 'We could do with somebody like her on our team – good technical knowledge is hard to find.' He avoided Gheeta's killing look which he knew would be aimed his way. 'So if she didn't stay here and didn't go back to your mother's, where do you think she spent the night?'

'No idea, sorry.' Cathy shrugged. 'But I wouldn't worry too much about her, she's a tough one is Sammy.'

Palmer thought better of telling Cathy that even being a 'tough one' wouldn't stop a 9mm bullet.

'Could I have her mobile number please?' Gheeta opened her laptop ready to input it.

'Yes, of course.' Cathy said the number as Gheeta posted it on an email and sent it to Claire with 'Sam's Mobile' as the post name.

'Thank you,' she said as it winged its way to the Claire.

'Right.' Palmer turned towards the door. 'Well, we won't take up anymore of your time.'

Gheeta held out a contact card. 'If she comes here, please tell her to get in touch.'

****

Trevor Black and Jerry Houseman got as far as the stairway landing that led off to the Lanes' flat before swiftly doing an about turn and hurrying back down. A landing full of uniformed and CSI officers was not what they wanted to meet. Their second visit to Sammy's mother would have to wait.

****

DAY 4

Gheeta was sitting at her terminal tapping the keyboard when Palmer walked into the Team Room the next morning. Next to her, Claire was doing likewise. He'd been waylaid by Lucy Price on his way in; Lucy handled the media and press department and had told him the balloon had gone up and there was a media feeding frenzy erupting about the case. Three bodies in an open grave was grist to the mill of any crime reporter, and the gravedigger had been talking to any of them that offered the king's shilling. It was likely to get a bit out of hand with lurid headlines, and Lucy wanted Palmer to give a press briefing later that day and cool it down. She would fix it up and let him know when.

After the usual 'good mornings' exchange Palmer took off his trilby and coat and looked at the progress board, where Gheeta had added the Lanes' flat address and blank spaces for the two men that called at Motörhead's.

'That gravedigger has been shouting his mouth off.' Palmer wasn't happy; he didn't like press briefings unless he had something positive to say, and so far nothing positive about this case had surfaced. 'Press briefing later – waste of time.'

'May not be, guv.' Gheeta gave him a smile, the smile that told him she was onto something.

Palmer moved across and stood behind the pair of them. 'Go on?'

'I was reading the Lanes' file at home last night and it lists a number of burglaries attributed to them but not proved, so no arrests or convictions followed. We know they had a habit of checking supermarket car parks and stealing dash cams, sat navs or anything else left in full view – a quick smash and grab and away.'

'Yes, with the owner well away inside the supermarket and out of the picture.' Palmer could see why the Lanes did that. 'Simple, quick and very sellable for cash, no questions asked.'

Gheeta nodded and continued. 'Yes, and how many of us take any notice of a car alarm going off in a big car park? Most people would ignore it.'

Palmer knew she was onto something and was impatient to know what. 'So cut to the chase, Sergeant.'

'Well, according to the file, the last car park raid with their name in the frame as the likely perpetrators was ten days ago at Morrison's in Camden. I took a look on my way in this morning – big store, big car park and big surveillance system, multiple CCTV covering the store and the car park. The manager was very helpful and has sent me a copy of the car park camera file of the day of the smash and grab. Take a look.'

Palmer stepped back and looked up at the large plasma screen on the wall above the row of Gheeta's various PCs and servers sat along the back of the desks. The screen flicked into action and showed an aerial view of the car park from the roof of the store. It was indeed a large car park. Gheeta moved the action along at speed and then slowed it to normal.

'Now, guv, top left.'

At the far end of the car park Palmer could just about make out three figures moving through the lines of parked cars and stopping beside one. After a few seconds, their jerky movements beside the car suggested an attack of some sort, and then they were running away, splitting up and leaving in different directions. Gheeta stopped the action.

'Look at the one on the left, he's carrying something shiny.'

Palmer could see it. 'A laptop – Sammy's laptop?'

'Could well be, guv. Now we switch to twenty minutes later and a different camera at the exit. The manager said the car owner was asked if she wanted the police called, and offered the use of the store's delivery bay round the back and some help in cleaning up the glass inside the car, but she declined both offers and then left without leaving any details. This is the car leaving.'

The screen showed a black Range Rover turning from the store's exit and moving out of the camera shot into the road. The side view was of the passenger side and showed an open gap where the window had been.

'So if the driver left no details, how comes it's on the Lanes' file at Hampstead nick?' Palmer asked.

'The store has a policy of reporting any disturbances or trouble to the local police in case there's any later comeback, and Hampstead nick is the nearest to the Camden Morrison's so they reported it there. Superintendent Hawkins's chaps picked up on it at their daily briefing as being the Lanes' MO and logged it on their file. No complaint from the driver so no further action. But it gets more interesting.' She pointed a finger towards Claire.

Palmer pulled up a seat from under the row of trestle tables on the other side of the

Team Room and sat between them as Claire took up the story.

'The Range Rover's plate is quite visible when the car leaves the supermarket, and according to the DVLA it belongs to Charmaine Day.'

'Doesn't ring a bell.' Palmer wondered what the significance of the name was.

'Daughter of Robert Day?' Gheeta turned and raised her eyebrows at Palmer. 'Any bells ringing now, sir?'

Palmer took in a deep breath. '*The* Robert Day?'

Gheeta nodded. 'Yes, *the* Robert Day. Owner's address is the same as the one on file for him. '

'Clue me in,' said Claire, swinging round in her chair. 'The name doesn't mean anything to me.'

Palmer sat back and folded his arms before giving Claire a potted history of Robert Day. He ended it with, 'If the Lanes nicked his laptop then their number was up as soon as they did it. Mr Day doesn't forgive.'

'Three killed and one on the run is a hefty price to pay for nicking a laptop. Must be a pretty important laptop,' Claire said.

Palmer agreed. 'Be nice to get to it before Day does and take a good look. I'll pop down and have a word with Peter Long, see if he can bring us up to date on Mr Day.'

****

Commander Peter Long ran the Organised Crime Squad, and like Palmer was a long serving officer of the old school type who had worked his way up through the ranks and refused early retirement or to be sidelined into a desk job. Also like Palmer, he had more clout with, and respect from, the people who matter at the Home Office than AC Bateman, and also often registered his disapproval of any plans to amalgamate OC with other departments. He and Palmer formed a twin attack every time the subject was mentioned. What Peter Long didn't know about the *who*, the *what*, and the *where* in organised crime in London wasn't worth knowing.

'Come in, Justin.' Long looked up at Palmer's knock on his glass office door set at the back of the noisy OC Team Room on the first floor. 'I've half been expecting you.'

Long was, as usual, immaculately dressed in a dark blue suit, light blue shirt, dark blue tie and black shoes shined to perfection. Any stranger walking into the OC Team Room populated with plain-clothed officers in a variety of old jeans, T-shirts and the occasional rumpled jacket street wear would have no difficulty in picking out *the boss*.

Palmer took a seat at Long's desk. 'You have?'

'Robert Day.' Long smiled. 'You can't keep things quiet when that bastard's involved. Found his laptop yet?'

Palmer gave a respectful nod. 'You *are* well informed, Peter. No, we haven't – we know who's got it but haven't traced her yet. What's on it, any idea?'

'Rumour has it there's a complete listing of all the bungs he's given to bent coppers and details of where he launders his ill-gotten gains. Heavy stuff.'

'Heavy enough to kill for.'

'Oh yes, if Internal Affairs got hold of it I have no doubt a few early retirements from the force would happen – probably some in my squad too, and Day would have no defence against a bribery and corruption charge.'

'So where can I find Mr Day?'

'Elusive character – keeps a low profile, but he has an office at the back of one of

74

his Chinese restaurants and takeaways in the Edgware Road. I wouldn't go unannounced if I were you, he doesn't take kindly to surprises. In fact, a better idea is if I put one of my chaps who knows all about Day and his associates into your team – safer that way.' Long stood and looked through the glass at the officers working at their desks and talking with each other in his busy team room. 'I seem to remember you worked with Knight once before, didn't you?

Palmer nodded. 'Yes, damn good officer too. Is he available?'

'I'll make him available.' Long walked round his desk to the door and called in Knight, a late-twenties slim officer with short dark hair, clean shaven, and, if Palmer remembered correctly, handy with his fists. 'DI Knight, you know DCS Palmer, Serial Murder Squad, don't you? You worked with his team once before.'

DI Knight nodded. 'Yes sir, I think that case ended up with DI Kirby getting four years for corruption and a takeaway off the Charing Cross road being blown up.' He nodded to Palmer. 'How are you, sir?'

Palmer laughed at the recollection of the case. 'I'm very well, Knight – can't promise you such excitement this time, but I'll do my best.'

Long sat back at his desk.

'Robert Day. You know all about him Knight, don't you?' asked Long.

Knight gave a resigned look. 'Oh yes, one of our *Teflon* group – nothing ever sticks to him. Every time we pull him in on something rock solid, alibis suddenly appear or the rock solid witnesses disappear or withdraw their statements. Done three raids on his various properties where good info says drugs are housed, and each time we came up empty. He's got contacts inside the force, but we've not been able to nail anybody. Nasty piece of work too.'

'Right, well delegate whatever you're working on at the moment to another of your team and work with DCS Palmer. From what he's told me we've a good chance of nailing Day this time. Pull out any information files on him and take them with you.' Long became very serious. 'Do it quietly, and not a word to anybody down here that it's Robert Day you're working on – his money buys a lot of self preservation as you well know, understand?'

Knight nodded. 'Understood.'

'Right then.' Palmer stood to leave and tapped Knight on the arm. 'I'll see you upstairs whenever you're ready.'

****

Lucy Price buttonholed Palmer on the stairs.

'Aha, got you – your sergeant said she thought you might have left the building.' Gheeta knew how Palmer hated press briefings and had spun a little white lie to Lucy; Lucy also knew how much he hated press briefings and knew it was a little white lie. 'You've got an hour before the press briefing in the Media Suite. Don't be late, I'm expecting a full house on this one – Bateman's leading it.'

Palmer raised his eyebrows. 'Bateman's leading it? He doesn't know anything about the case.'

'He knows three lads have been killed with a bullet in their heads and he knows all the TV channels will be there, so Bateman will be there.' She gave Palmer a knowing smile. 'I wonder why?'

Palmer returned it, knowing full well why Bateman would be there, as did Lucy. AC Bateman relished the TV cameras, knowing their coverage of him on the news would be viewed by his Home Office superiors, the ones who would be responsible for choosing the next Commissioner when the time came. If there was a Phd in *Brown-nosing,* Bateman would have passed it with honours!

Lucy gave Palmer a stern look. 'An hour, Justin – don't be late.'

She went down, he went up.

****

Trevor Black was puffing a bit after climbing the stairs to Motörhead's balcony.

'Why haven't they got a bloody lift? Bugger living up here.'

Houseman laughed. He'd taken the steps two at a time and was waiting. 'You're getting old, Trevor, we both are – just that I've aged better than you.'

'Oh yeah? Who's the one who falls asleep in the car when we're watching a place then, eh?'

'A quick forty winks, that's all.'

'You don't snore when you're having forty winks.'

They walked along the balcony, noting crime scene tape over the doorway to the Lanes' flat.

'I take it the magicians went in?'

'Yes, straight away.'

Black had to knock twice on Motörhead's door before she opened it with the chain firmly on.

'I ain't talking to you. You ain't coppers, you lied to me.'

'You never asked if we were police, I didn't lie. Has Samantha been back?'

'None of your business – piss off.' She tried to shut the door, but Black had already positioned his shoe as a stop.

'Has she?'

'Take your foot away, I've nothing to say to you.'

The foot stayed in place.

'Has she rung you? Do you know where she is?'

'I'm calling the police.'

Motörhead left the door and walked back down the hallway making for her mobile on the kitchen table. Behind her the force of Black's right shoe against the door sent it flying open and the chain and slide bouncing down the hall after her. She turned to be met by Black's right fist smashing into her chin. She went out like a light and slumped to the floor.

Houseman shut the front door and wedged it shut with a broken child's bike that was stood against the hall wall. He bent over Motörhead and checked in her mouth. If she had false teeth they could have been knocked down her throat and could suffocate her. She had her own teeth; smoke-stained, but her own.

'Right, let's see what we can find then.' Black took a pair of latex gloves from his pocket and pulled them on as Houseman did the same. 'Anything that can give us a clue where this bloody girl is, or better still the fucking laptop itself.'

****

Both Gheeta and Claire were pleased to be working with Knight again.

'Do we have to call you 'sir' now you're a DI?' Gheeta asked with a smile.

Knight thought for a moment. 'Well, seeing that I got the promotion after a successful period of work with you lot last time I don't think so. Knight will do just fine. Where's the boss?'

'Press briefing. Bateman's there, so he's not going to be '*happy Larry*' when he comes back.'

They sat round a trestle table as Gheeta brought Knight up to speed on the case.

Her mobile rang. 'Hello, DS Singh... Who?... Sorry, can't understand you – who is it?... Oh, Mrs Johnson – you sound like you've got a mouthful of cake... You've what?... When?... Okay, stay there. I'll be with you as soon as I can.' She clicked off the phone and explained the call. 'Mrs Johnson. Our two men looking for Samantha made a repeat visit and it sounds like they roughed her up a bit – we'd better get over there. Claire, tell the guv what's happened when he gets back, I'll call in as soon as I can assess the situation. Ring down and get a car to the front for us. Come on, Knight – duty calls. This squad doesn't sit around in their Team Room drinking coffee all day.' She picked up her shoulder bag and, putting her laptop inside, was off out of the door.

'Cheeky bitch.' Knight gave Claire a wave and followed.

****

81

The media suite was packed, just as Lucy had said it would be. Nothing like a good *gangland murder* to get a crime correspondent's juices running! Palmer had to push through a crowded doorway on his way in.

Most of the established journalists knew him and their despondent attitude to a press briefing with AC Bateman, known as *'boring Bateman'* in press circles, was lifted when they saw Palmer arrive.

'Thank God you're doing it, Justin,' said Charlie Moores of the *Standard* as Palmer brushed past him. 'At least we'll get some real information on what's happening.'

'Not a lot to tell yet, Charlie.' Palmer gave him a smile. 'But I'll do my best to give you a headline.'

Stepping onto the small briefing room platform with the Union Jack and the Met's insignia flag hanging on the wall behind, Palmer nodded to Bateman as Lucy set out the agenda to the media.

Bateman leant close to Palmer. 'I'll do a quick resume of the facts, Palmer, then over to you.'

'Right-o, sir.' Palmer wondered what facts Bateman knew, other than that three youths had been found dead in an open grave and the investigation was ongoing.

And that was about it. Bateman smoothed over his bald pate with a tissue so the camera lights didn't reflect off it, made sure his tie was straight, spoke directly towards the TV cameras and said that three youths had been found dead in an open grave and the investigation was ongoing. 'Now I'll hand over to DCS Palmer, who is OIC of the case.'

Palmer took the media through the case, mentioning the details he wanted to mention and withholding those he didn't. He told them it was probably a gangland killing because the bullets matched those already on the police data bank at NABIS, the National Ballistics Intelligence Service, so the general public had no need to worry unduly about their personal safety. He told them his squad were looking for a young lady called Samantha Johnson who they thought might be in danger, and a photo would be issued from the press and media department in due course. He fielded questions about whether it was drugs-related, saying that it wasn't known at this time, and basically gave the media enough for a good headline but not enough to set them off on their own investigations; except for giving them the

Lanes' names, which would send the investigative journalists off on a hunt to find out more about them, whilst Palmer's team could concentrate on Robert Day. He didn't mention Day or the two men at Motörhead's flat. He made a mental note to remind Motörhead not to speak to the media as it could jeopardise Samantha's safety.

****

'Look at the mess they made, and look at my mouth.' Motörhead mumbled the words, pointing at her swollen lips in a cracked wall mirror hanging perilously from a bent nail in her hall. Gheeta thought about telling her it was all the rage amongst the young Z-list female celebrities at the moment to have duck lips, and that an injection of Botox to achieve the same result as a punch from Black would cost her a fortune. But she didn't.

'Is anything missing?' she asked. 'Has Samantha been back?'

'No, and if you're thinking of that laptop neither her nor it have been back. I would have rung you if she had.'

Gheeta didn't know whether to believe that or not.

'Recognise these two, Mrs Johnson?' Knight showed her colour mugshots of Black and Houseman. 'I think these two may have been your visitors.'

Motörhead nodded. 'Bloody right they were – arrest them and charge them with assault. Attacking an old lady in her own home, outrageous.'

Knight gave her a smile. 'Where's the old lady they attacked? I haven't seen an old lady in here.'

Motörhead gave Gheeta a knowing look. 'He's a smooth one isn't he, eh?'

'I couldn't possibly comment, Mrs Johnson. Now, I think we'll get a car to pop you down to the local hospital for an X-ray – that jaw is quite swollen.'

'I'm not going anywhere, take more than some bully boy to hospitalise me. The swelling will go down in a day or two.'

'Alright, but I'll get one of our contractors to come round later and put a proper security lock on your door. Now, if we could go and sit down somewhere I have to take a statement from you about the assault.'

'Okay, and I'll fill in a claim form too.'

'A claim form?'

'From the victims' compensation fund – I might have lifelong mental problems as a result of that terrible attack.'

****

A little later back in the Team Room Knight went through the Robert Day folder with Palmer and the team.

'Mrs Johnson identified these two as her assailants.' He pulled out the 10 x 8s of Black and Houseman. 'Two people we know quite well in OC – a couple of quite nasty heavies, violence for hire and thought to be involved in more than a few gangland hits and disappearances. NABIS has a trace on them through their ammunition.' He pulled out a basic map of the UK with bright red crosses marked on several places. 'The crosses mark places where the same guns have been used in woundings and killings, as revealed by analysis of the bullets recovered from the scenes or taken out of the bodies at the post mortems. We call this the Red Cross case, purely and simply because that's about all we have on the killings – a red cross on a map.'

'Couldn't the guns be rental guns shifted around and used by different gangs and people? Why just Black and Houseman?' Palmer asked.

'At four of the incidents positive IDs of Black and Houseman had been made by independent witnesses, so it's pretty reasonable to assume they were involved, knowing what their business is. In each case those witnesses have since withdrawn their identifications and failed to pick out either Black or Houseman in line-ups. So obviously threats have been made.'

'Right. Get around a bit this Black and Houseman don't they?' Palmer pointed around the map. 'Manchester, Glasgow, Birmingham, Leeds, four crosses in London – popular pair, are they?'

Knight nodded. 'Professional, very professional. We think the four London killings were ordered and paid for by Robert Day. Our information from the street was that all four were pushing into Day's turf with drug dealing – not a very intelligent move.'

'Right, so Black and Houseman are our main target then. We've got Motörhead's positive ID and the CCTV from number 92's bell...'

Knight interrupted him. 'Motörhead?'

Gheeta explained. 'It's the guv's nickname for Mrs Johnson. Didn't you notice the T-shirt?'

Knight laughed. 'No, can't say I did.'

Palmer ignored the interruption and pointed to the pictures of Black and Houseman. 'These two are our murder suspects, so Mr Day will have to take a back seat for the present – hopefully what we dig up on them will incriminate Day as well, but at the moment we need to get after Black and Houseman. Right, where do we start? If they are after the girl Samantha then we need to get to her first.'

'And get to the laptop first, guv,' said Gheeta. 'That seems to be the Pandora's box that Day doesn't want opened, and wants back so badly he sends out killers to find it.'

'We could put surveillance on them, see what they're up to and where they are going?' suggested Knight.

'No, we need to be ahead of them. We need to have been to all the places they're likely to go to before them. This Samantha obviously knows that the laptop is very special to somebody, so where would she go to make contact with the owner and ask for money? I take it she has no idea who Robert Day is?'

'She might do – and anyway, after the three killings she must have cottoned on to the fact that whoever owns it is not to be messed with, guv,' said Gheeta. 'She's seen three of her family of thieves killed for it, so she's not likely to broadcast that she's got it, is she?'

Knight pointed to Black and Houseman's pictures. 'Her only way to contact the owner and make a demand for money for its return is through these two – they are the only way she has to contact the owner.'

'Even if she saw them at the Lanes' flat, I don't think she'd know who they are or want to make contact with them, do you?' said Palmer. 'Let's face it, if you saw three mates being killed for a laptop you'd hardly poke your head above the parapet and say 'Here it is, I've got it and want some money for it', would you?'

'No, 'Gheeta agreed. 'So she's stuck in a corner, isn't she? She can't sell it to those who want it because they'll just kill her and take it.'

'She needs a go-between.' Palmer rubbed his chin in thought. 'Who did the Lanes fence their stuff through?'

'Depends what it was,' explained Knight. 'Plenty of antique dealers, coin dealers, watch shops and the like more than ready to buy for cash and ask no questions if the price is low enough. Computer stuff and laptops would have gone to pawn shops mainly, but if she knows what's on it is worth a lot more than the basic second-hand value she's not going to offload it to any of those, is she? We also have a suspicion that the Lane's probation officer isn't totally straight – nothing definite, but stakeouts on other people and places involved in moving stolen goods have reported him showing up on more than one occasion. She might use him if our suspicions are right and the Lanes used him.'

'Henry Gooch?' Palmer asked.

'Yes, that's him. You know him?'

'He came in and gave us the Lanes' and Smith's probation records in case there was anything in them of interest.'

'And was there?'

'No, nothing. So maybe his visit was an attempt to get himself out of the picture?'

Palmer thought for a moment. 'Samantha Johnson will know those places the Lanes usually sold to are under the radar and would be known to other criminals for taking stolen goods, so they might well have been told

90

already to look out for this laptop by the owner or Black and Houseman and to call in if it's offered. Right, let's start there then. We need to pay a visit to all the pawn shops, Cash Converter type shops and the like, starting at those nearest to the Lanes' estate and work outwards. Make sure that if this laptop is offered to anybody we get the call, not Day or his henchmen.'

'Going to want a couple more officers to help on that guv, or we'll be doing it for months,' Gheeta said.

Palmer agreed. 'I'll have a word with Bateman. Have a ring round and see who's available.'

When required Palmer was able to bring in experienced officers to assist in his squad's cases. Gheeta had a list of those tried and tested officers who would jump at the chance if they were on leave or owed days off; they'd get overtime rates, although the prospect of working with Palmer far outweighed the monetary gain. His outspoken, no nonsense way of policing greatly appealed to a lot in the force in these times of political correctness, and certainly appealed to the majority of the public who felt that the criminal aggressor had more human rights than the victim.

****

Palmer stood in front of AC Bateman's neatly arranged minimalistic desk in Bateman's neatly arranged minimalistic office on the 5th Floor. Bateman's desk certainly gave credence to the well-worn joke amongst the lower ranks that the ACs spent all day re-arranging the paperclips on their desks and choosing between custard creams or digestives to have with their numerous cups of tea. The opposite was true of Palmer's office desk, which resembled an offspring of the local tip; as did his whole office, even though Gheeta tidied it every morning.

Bateman frowned. 'How many extra officers?'

'Just two, sir. We've got a lot of legwork coming up and I think time is of the essence to get round the people we need to talk to before we get any more bodies turning up.'

The thought of more bodies turning up wasn't one Bateman wanted to contemplate. The powers above were already demanding progress on the case. Postcode gang drug dealers knifing each other in East London had become par for the course with the media and hardly mentioned these days, but three youths shot in the head and dumped in an open grave didn't give out a good image for the Home Office and Home Secretary who had managed to keep the growing prevalence of guns being used amongst the capital's criminals low key up to now. It was a no-brainer; even so Bateman's money-conscious mind, that worried more about budgets than arrests, was fighting his sensible reaction to let Palmer have the officers.

He took a deep breath and spread his hands in a resigned manner. 'Okay, Palmer, two only – and keep them for as few days as you can, budgets are very tight, very tight indeed.'

'Cancel HSB2, sir – be able to double the force then. Ask the Home Secretary to have a word with the clown in Downing Street.' Palmer liked to get a political jab in when he could.

'Yes, thank you, Palmer. Anything else?' Bateman was used to Palmer's jabs and dismissed it without comment.

'No, sir – oh, just to say thank you for your input to the press briefing earlier. Much appreciated.'

Bateman brightened. 'Oh, really? Well, thank you, Palmer. I didn't say much.'

'No, sir, that's why it was much appreciated.'

Palmer turned and left quickly before Bateman could think of a way to put him on a charge of insubordination.

****

Gheeta had no trouble in pulling in two additions to the team as soon as Palmer told her Bateman had sanctioned it. She poked her head round his office door where he was looking through the Lanes' probation reports again, just in case any other relevant facts had been missed on the first read.

'We've got Simms and Lewis joining us tomorrow, guv.'

Palmer thought for a moment, checking his memory. 'Lewis, is that the WPC from Greenwich area?' He stood and followed Gheeta across the corridor into the Team Room where Claire and Knight were working.

Gheeta nodded. 'That's the one – worked with us on the Felt Tip Murders case. She's a DS now.'

'Is she? Good for her. Right then, in the morning get started with the pawnbrokers and second-hand shops that we know will turn a blind eye to stolen stuff – see if we can't find out if Samantha is hawking that laptop around.'

'If the word is out that Robert Day is after it, they'll give it a miss if she did offer it,' Knight said. 'He's the kind of bloke you just don't want to get involved with in any way, and he certainly won't pay anybody for finding it. Being grateful isn't in his work ethic.'

Palmer nodded. He was not liking this Robert Day character one bit; in fact the more he heard about him, the more he disliked him. 'Sergeant, in the morning you and Knight take a panda car and go into Day's home turf in Hampstead and stir it up a bit. Be very visible and start asking about '*a girl with a laptop*', see if we can't get a little panic going with Mr Day. If there's stuff on that laptop that he wants so badly that he'll kill for it let him know through the street grapevine that we are looking for it too. It might push him into a mistake.'

****

DAY 5

Samantha Johnson took a quick morning shower in the Lanes' empty flat. It had struck her the afternoon before that nobody would ever think of looking for her there. It was a crime scene with blue and white tape strung over the doorway and a police no entry sign.

She had spent the day in the West End well away from home turf, wandering around the National Gallery and window shopping on the Strand and Bond Street. Depending on how much money she got for the laptop's return, she might treat herself. In reality she knew she wouldn't; once a Primark shopper, always a Primark shopper. She smiled at the thought of her mother's face if she turned up with a Versace bag. The whole block would know within ten minutes, and most of them would be sure she'd stolen it.

She had a meal in a crowded KFC and when darkness had fallen had made her way back to the estate and stood between the large council refuse bins opposite the block for half an hour, just making sure nobody was waiting and watching her mother's flat. Then, when she was satisfied all was clear, she'd made her way to the Lanes' flat and opened the door, stepped through the criss-crossed crime scene tape stretched across it, slipped quickly inside and closed it behind her, putting on the chain. She thought about ringing her mum just to say she was safe and switched on her mobile. Then she had second thoughts; mum would ask too many questions. She switched it off again. Anger rose inside as she saw the bloodstains on the sofa. She lay on George's bed and drifted off to sleep, after shedding a few tears as the years of friendship with the boys and the fun times flitted across her memory.

She dried herself after the shower and checked she'd not left any clues to her having been in the flat. She knew exactly what her next move was going to be, and waited until the morning commute hubbub in the estate was over before sneaking out and away to rent a car and set her plan into action.

****

At the daily morning meeting in the Team Room Gheeta brought Lewis and Simms up to speed with the case and issued all the team with squad iPhones that Claire had uploaded with Day, Black and Houseman mugshots and the picture of Samantha Johnson that she had downloaded at Motörhead's flat. Gheeta and Knight took the panda car out to start stirring things up on the street and Lewis and Simms left in separate plain cars to watch Day's restaurant in Hampstead High Street for any action happening there. Lewis took the front and Simms parked up in the back street behind the restaurant that gave a clear view of the narrow back access lane to the rear of the row of businesses the restaurant was in.

****

It didn't take long on the street for Gheeta and Knight to sense something unusual was going on. When the fourth known fence operating either an antique shop or pawnbrokers had shut up like a clam at the mention of a laptop being offered, Knight decided it was time to open a mouth and they headed to a small back street pawnbrokers round the back of the Dunboyne Estate in Highgate. Council estates had always provided good business for pawnbrokers, legal or not.

A mild look of fear crossed the owner Randall Harrington's face as he looked through the counter grille and saw Knight and Gheeta enter his shop.

'No warrant no search.' This was his automatic response to any visit from the police or Customs and Excise, and he'd had quite a few visits in the past from both.

'Tut, tut, tut, Randall,' said Knight with a smile. 'Why on earth would you think we wanted to search the premises? Don't tell me you've got something out the back that you shouldn't have?' He added, raising his eyebrows questioningly, 'Surely not?'

'There's nothing on the premises that I haven't got a legal receipt for, Mr Knight.'

'Glad to hear that, Randall. How about a laptop that seems to be causing some excitement?'

Silence.

'Been offered to you, has it?' Knight held Randall's eyes in a cold glare.

Still silence.

'Okay, Randall, I'll ask my partner here to phone in and get a search warrant and a closure order put on these premises, as I have a strong suspicion that you have items here of great interest to the police.'

It took a few seconds for Harrington to realise Knight was serious. And indeed,

Harrington did have a few items that would interest the police. He played it cagey. 'What laptop?'

'You know exactly what laptop, Randall. If it makes you feel better, this conversation is off the record between you and me. Robert Day's laptop.'

Harrington nodded. 'Well, you already know its Day's, so I won't be telling you anything you don't already know, will I? Yes his boys have been round threatening everybody and saying that if it's offered to get it at all costs and let them know.' He lowered his voice. 'It's tied up with the Lane boys' murders, isn't it? The buzz in the business is that it's got a lot of info on it about Day's business and contacts, including those from your side of the fence. Three kids dead already, so nobody's going to get involved if they can help it are they.'

'Has it been hawked round?'

'I don't think so. Nobody I know in the business has been offered it as far as I know. To be honest, Mr Knight, if it came in here I'd refuse it. One bloke I wouldn't want to be mixed up with in any way is Robert Day – no thank you.'

'Okay, Randall, I actually believe you for once, if it does appear anywhere let me know, won't you?' Knight knew that Harrington wouldn't.

'Of course.'

'My colleague has the contact number.'

Gheeta slid a card under the grille.

Harrington looked at it. 'Serial Murder Squad – you changed departments, Mr Knight?

'No, Randall, just giving a helping hand. I'll be back with OC giving you hassle again when this is sorted.'

'I can't wait,' said Harrington in a sarcastic way.

****

It took twenty minutes for Claire to register Samantha Johnson's phone on the monitoring system and get a printout of the last calls that spilled from the printer. She took it across the corridor to Palmer's office where he was signing off the personnel department documents transferring the wage time sheets for Knight, Lewis and Simms to his department budget.

Claire gave a tap at the door; nobody else did, most just barged in and Palmer had given up remonstrating. It made no difference.

He looked up. 'Come in, Claire. What have you found?'

She put the printout on his desk in front of him. 'Samantha Johnson hardly ever uses her phone, sir. It's off most of the time – but she switched it on last night at 11.32pm.'

'Who did she call?'

'She didn't, she switched it off again without making a call. But we can pinpoint her position from the interpolation between the four nearest masts.'

'Where was she?'

'In the Bevan estate, sir – in the same block as the Lanes' flat and her mother's.'

Palmer thought for a few moments. 'You know, I bet she spent the night in the Lanes' flat. She wouldn't go to her mum's, she'd get too much grief and hassle from her, and Black and Houseman might pay a second visit. No, I reckon the crafty young lady sneaked into the Lanes' for the night. Nobody would think of looking there for her. She's a clever little so and so, isn't she? Right, give Superintendent Hawkins a bell and explain it to him and ask for a quick forensic check on the place. No calls from her phone since, are there?'

'No, sir, it's been off all the time. I've keyed in our computer to the monitoring system, so we'll get an immediate notification if it comes online.'

****

Henry Gooch sat at his desk in the council offices writing a report on the last of his probation charges who had just left the room. He checked his watch: 12.30, lunchtime, no more appointments until 2pm when the next one was due to report; time to wander out and get a sandwich. He stood up from the desk and stopped dead still as the door opened and Samantha Johnson came in, quickly shutting the door behind her and clicking the lock. He had never met Samantha before – yes, he'd seen her come with George Lane and wait for George in the waiting room and then leave with him, but they'd never spoken. He sat back down and waited for Samantha to open the conversation. How much did she know about Henry Gooch and his business on the side?

Samantha walked across the large office and stood the other side of the desk.

'You know who I am, don't you, Mr Gooch?'

'Yes.'

Samantha put the Tesco bag she was carrying on the desk and pushed it across to Gooch.

'And you know what that is, don't you, Mr Gooch.' It was a statement of fact, not a question.

Gooch opened the bag and looked at the laptop inside.

'Yes.'

Word travels fast in the criminal world and some of his *clients* had already mentioned the Lanes and the hunt for Day's laptop.

'You always got a fair price for anything George brought you to sell for him, so I'd like you to get a fair price for that, Mr Gooch – and I mean a fair price. The information on that will put Robert Day away for a long time if it ends up in police hands. Day knows that and killed my friends to get it back. That wasn't a nice thing to do, Mr Gooch, and has to be paid for. Start at fifty grand and see how that interests Day. I think that's fair – I reckon that two grand for every year he'd spend inside if it ends up in police hands is fair. I'll be in touch, Mr Gooch.'

And with that Samantha Johnson turned to leave the office. She stopped after she had opened the door and looked back at Gooch.

'No double crossing me, Mr Gooch. I've left a note about your little sideline in good hands. If anything happens to me, it goes to the police.'

With that warning she left and closed the door behind her.

Gooch slid the laptop out of the bag; he sat and thought for while, his mind going over his options. A call to Robert Day offering the laptop? But should he say he'd got it or he could get it? If he told Day he'd got it Day would take it, and then would he get the money for it that Samantha wanted? Probably not. What if he said he could get his hands on it? Day would probably tell him to go ahead and get a meeting organised with Samantha, that wasn't possible; she was too streetwise to meet Day.

He thought some more; he'd prefer to have an angry Samantha than an angry Robert Day – and after all, he had done a lot of business over the years with Day, and he'd like that to continue. However, as Samantha had said, three were dead already for knowing the contents of this laptop; what was to stop Day getting it back and having him killed? Obviously what was on it was mega important, and Day wasn't taking chances on anybody who might have looked at it talking, and that would include him, even if he swore he hadn't had a look. Gooch knew enough about computers to know that any access to the laptop would be registered on it; so if he rang Day now and Day checked it, there wouldn't be any access registered whilst it was in his possession. Yes, that was the best idea. He made the call.

Day answered almost immediately.

'I told you not ring me, I ring you.'

'I have something you want.'

'My county lines full; I ring you if I need any of your young offenders to plug gap. I ring you, you understand?'

'I have a laptop you might be interested in.'

There was a silence for a short time.

'You sure it right one?'

'Dell Inspiron15.'

'Where you get it?'

'The young lady you're looking for brought it in.'

'Why she bring to you?'

'I was the Lanes' probation officer.'

'The Lanes?'

'Three bodies in a grave.'

'I get it picked up right away.'

'She wants sixty grand in cash.' Gooch wanted something for his trouble.

106

'Need to make sure it right one first. You had a look?'

'No.'

'You sure about that?'

'What I don't know can't hurt me.'

'Yes, stick to that if I were you. Black will be over to pick it up. Stay put.'

Click, the phone went dead.

****

Samantha Johnson sat in the rented Fiesta opposite the council offices. She was waiting for Gooch to hurry out and take the laptop to Day, which she was pretty sure he would do. She would follow and find out where Day was, and then plan a way of killing him. Time went by with plenty of movement in and out of the building, but not Gooch. It was lunch hour, so could she have missed him? Perhaps he had brought sandwiches and had them in the office? Then she saw it. The laptop, still in the Tesco bag, held firmly under the arm of a smartly dressed man in his early forties who left the building with another man; they crossed road, dodging between the traffic, stopped at a red light and got into the passenger seat of a

Lexus parked a few cars in front of her. She had mildly noticed it when it had pulled in and parked earlier but hadn't paid it much attention; now all her attention was on it as it pulled out and made off down the road with her following a few cars back.

****

'Lewis to base.'

DS Lewis's voice came over the comms wall speaker in the Team Room.

'Go ahead, Lewis,' Claire answered as Palmer came in, having heard the call across in his office.

'Black and Houseman have just gone into Day's restaurant in the Edgware road. Black had what looks like the laptop under his arm in a bag.'

Claire looked to Palmer for instructions.

'Tell her to stay there, see if anything happens. At least we know where it is now.'

Claire passed the order on.

'Right, hold the fort, Claire – I'm going up to Bateman to get a warrant to seize that laptop whilst we can. It's obviously material evidence in the murder of the three boys.'

He left the Team Room and at the end of the corridor took the stairs up two at a time – well, he took the first four stairs two at a time, and then the stab of sciatica in his right thigh told him to take the rest one at a time, which he did.

****

'Ha! It home at last.' Robert Day smiled at the laptop on his desk. 'Well done, well done, boys.' He flashed a smile at Black and Houseman. 'Gooch, he any trouble?'

Black laughed. 'None. He won't be troubling you for any money either.'

'That shame really, he useful from time to time. But I not risk him having take look.'

'He swore he hadn't.'

'Good, let's take look then – that tell me if he did or not. All on register.'

'Register?' Houseman didn't have much clue about computers.

'Yes, every time somebody log in it list it, page and time. Gooch ring about one o'clock, I make note, so any login after and it him.'

Day opened the laptop and pressed the start button.

'It's not starting.'

'Flat battery?' Black knew a little more about computers than Houseman.

'Yes, probably.' Day pulled the mains lead from a drawer and plugged it into the laptop, then pushed the plug into a wall socket and pressed the start button again. Nothing.

'That light at front should go on when it plugged in mains – something not right. Go get Azaff the waiter, he know all about computers – he scam silly women out of lot of money on computer. He know what to do.'

Houseman left and returned two minutes later with Azaff the waiter, who had a look of fear on his face. Day was one of those bosses who you didn't want to call you into his office. Azaff had seen a cashier who skimmed a little money off each bill be summoned to Day's office, and he hadn't been seen since.

'Azaff.' Day gave him a smile. 'This laptop no start, what I do wrong?'

Azaff checked the mains lead and pressed various keys and the mains light went on and the screen lit up light blue. And light blue it stayed. Azaff tapped away, but nothing, just a blue screen. He picked up the laptop and gave Day a worried look.

'It's inside, something's not right. Hang on.' He disappeared back into the restaurant and returned quickly with a small Pozidriv screwdriver and removed the back of the laptop. 'No hard drive.'

'What?' Day was panicking. 'What that, what hard drive?'

'It's the main thing, the part that holds all the information – the laptops's useless without it. It's been taken out.'

Day's expression hardened. 'Fucking Gooch.'

'Nah.' Black shook his head. 'Gooch hadn't the balls to do that, no way. It's gotta be the girl, that Samantha girl – she's taken it out as insurance that you'll pay the money. Stands to reason, she lets the laptop go to you so you know it's the right one and hangs onto the bit inside, whatever it's called...'

'Hard drive,' said Azaff.

'Yeah, the hard drive. She's going to hang onto it until you give Gooch the money and he passes it to her – crafty bitch. She's got it.'

'Well Gooch no going to get any cash now, so what she do? If she hands to police the shit really hit fan.'

'She won't, too much money involved to just back out. Me and Jerry will have words with her mother, she's bound to contact her sometime. Her mum might have a recent picture of the girl I can nab too. I'll put a reward out on the street for anybody letting me know where she is. Come on, Jerry.'

He left the back office, followed by Houseman, and they wound their way through the busy restaurant, swerving and barging between the customers queuing for takeaways.

'Oops – sorry, love.' Black collided with a girl in the queue who fell against Houseman. 'You alright?'

'Yes, I'm okay.'

They left the restaurant and hurried across the road to the car and drove off.

****

'Lewis to base.'

'Come in, Lewis,' Claire answered.

'Black and Houseman have left the restaurant and are off in the Lexus. I'm following.'

'Understood, Lewis. The boss is not in the office at present, but I'll get back to you as soon as he returns.'

'Copy that, base. Lewis out.'

****

Samantha Johnson left the takeaway queue and walked through the bustling restaurant to the door and watched Black and Houseman drive off. She felt the PPK that she had slipped from Houseman's shoulder holster when she had accidently on purpose fallen into him. It wouldn't be long surely before he noticed it was missing and they came back? She made her way to the ladies and shut herself in a cubicle and checked the gun; it had a full six clip of 9mm bullets in place but no silencer. Not a problem. She turned it over in her gloved hands; first thing she had done on every job with the Lanes was to put on her thin leather gloves, it became as natural to her as 'clunk-click'. Sammy's fingerprints weren't on anything, especially not the police database.

Walking from the ladies she made her way through the customers to the office door at the back of the restaurant. She had seen the man she'd taken the gun from come out and then go back in with a member of staff earlier, so she knew it was not locked. Her heart rate was accelerating through anger, not fear, as she opened the door and walked in.

****

'Simms to base.'

'Go ahead, Simms.'

'Something's happening inside the restaurant – the kitchen staff have just come running out the back in a bit of a panic. I'm going to take a look.'

'Palmer here, Simms. Are you armed?'

'No, sir.'

'Stay where you are until we get an armed response unit to you. Robert Day is not the sort that you want to come across unarmed.'

'Copy that. I'm parked at the entrance to the delivery road at the back of the shops.'

'Okay. Lewis, anything happening with your targets?'

'No, sir, still driving away – looks like they are heading for the Bevan estate.'

'Okay, stick with them. Base out.'

Palmer turned to Claire. 'Get onto SCO19 and get an ARV to Simms.'

'Will do.'

The internal telephone buzzed. Claire answered it.

'Superintendent Hawkins for you, sir.' She handed the receiver across.

'Palmer here... Hello, Hawkins... Yes... Okay... Yes I know, something's going on inside... I've got a man at the back who reported the staff rushing out from the place and we are getting an ARV unit to attend... Yes, you do that, but don't go in until the back-up arrives... Okay.' He gave the receiver back to Claire who replaced it on the wall unit and dialled the despatch room to ask for the ARV to be sent to Simms. Palmer picked up the comms microphone. 'Palmer to all units, there's a lot of 999 calls coming in about a shooting in Day's restaurant and Superintendent Hawkins is sending a uniformed TSG unit to secure the perimeter. We have an ARV unit going to liaise with Simms. DS Singh, you and Knight had better get over there and take control if there's an IOC. Simms, we now have a warrant to seize the laptop as material evidence in a murder case, so shut the place down and don't let any uniforms stomp all over it. I'll get Reg Frome to send a CSI unit and I'll get a car over myself. Palmer out.'

.

****

'My gun!'

'What?' Black turned to Houseman sitting beside him in the passenger seat.

Houseman was frantically looking on the car floor. 'My fucking gun is gone!'

'What do you mean *gone*?'

'Gone, that's what I mean – it's not in the shoulder holster. Somebody's had it.'

They looked at each other as the penny dropped.

'That fucking girl who bumped you in the queue, she was a dip. Fucking Samantha Johnson I bet!' Black pulled the car into the kerb, until a gap in the traffic let him squeal it round and head back to the restaurant.

****

'Lewis to base.'

'Go ahead, Lewis.' Palmer had left the Team Room to get a car to the restaurant and Claire answered.

'My targets have done an about turn, and judging by their speed they're aware of something happening at the restaurant and hurrying back there. Lewis out.'

'Did you get that, sir?' Although Claire had opened up the comms so that they could all hear and reply to the radio traffic, she wasn't sure Palmer had logged in. He had.

'Yes, got that. Lewis, make your way back – keep your cover so don't race after them or they'll make you. Liaise with Simms if you get there before DS Singh. Nobody goes inside until the ARV arrives, clear?'

'Clear, sir.'

'Simms, are the staff still around?'

'Yes, I've made them aware that I'm a police officer and they are not to go back inside. The 999 calls were correct, seems two gunshots were fired in the back office – Day's office. There's a delivery parking place behind the restaurant and then a high gate out to the access lane. I've shut the gate to keep them here for statements as most look like immigrants, and no doubt some will be illegals and will want to disappear quickly if I let them out.'

'Good lad, well done. Let them know we are not Immigration – we have no interest in that and they can go once we get their statements.'

****

Palmer stepped out of the squad car in front of the restaurant. The area had been taped off with crime scene tape and Hawkins had pulled in motorcycle officers from Traffic Division to close the Edgware Road at the first crossroads either side of the restaurant, to divert traffic and keep pedestrians well away. The shops either side had been cleared of staff and the managers or owners put behind the row of police cars and TSG and ARV unit minibuses.

Gheeta came over. 'I've taken IOC status, guv, and ARV have sent their men inside entering from both front and rear. Their control is Sergeant Hamp, he's over by the minibus.'

Palmer looked over and saw a fully kitted ARO speaking into his comms. He walked over with Singh. The ARO saluted, not something Palmer liked much; he was in the police, not the army. He didn't salute back.

'Palmer, Serial Murder Squad,' he introduced himself. 'Anything happening, Hamp?' The officer's name was on an embroidered name tag sewn onto his left jacket pocket.

'All quiet so far, sir. We have two units inside. Just lots of broken crockery and food on the floor where the customers fled knocking the tables over – same round the back in the kitchens, bit of a mess.' He held a finger up as a message came in to his ear. 'Okay, Two – move through and join One. You hear that, One?... Good, both units exit by the front.' He took his earpiece out. 'One dead body in the back office, sir – looks like he's been shot. My lads are coming out now, the place is secure – there's no other exits and the flats above are not connected to the restaurant premises, so nobody went that way. All clear.'

'Good, thank you, Hamp.' He turned to Gheeta. 'Sign off the ARU please, Sergeant, and get the TSG to secure the boundaries until Frome arrives with his chaps. No entry.'

Sergeant Singh went off to relay the instructions.

'Simms to Palmer.'

Palmer had forgotten about Simms sitting round the back. 'Go ahead, Simms.'

'I've got a chap here who has some info on what happened, and also what's on the laptop. If you can get a couple of uniforms to come round and make sure the rest of them don't do a runner, I'll bring him round.'

'Knight here, sir,' Knight interrupted the call. 'If that chap is called Azaff, let me go and get him. I know him and he knows me – I'm more likely to get the real truth out of him as I've enough on him to put him away for a few years if he doesn't cough.'

'What elite company you do keep, Knight. Simms, did you hear that?'

'Simms here – yes, copy that.'

'Okay, Simms, I'll get Sergeant Lewis to join you when she's back and both of you start questioning the staff. Leave the formal interviews to Hawkins's officers, just get a description of the killer or killers if you can. You hear that, Lewis? What's happening with you?'

'Parked up beyond the road barrier, sir. Black and Houseman parked their car in the kerb and are having a word with the motorcycle chaps at the tape. Lewis out.'

Palmer shot a look towards the tape but couldn't pick anybody out amongst the excited throng which was rapidly growing in number. 'Okay, leave them and join Simms please. We have the registration number so ANPR can keep track of them – and anyway, we don't have anything firm that we can use to pull them in for questioning at the moment, and we know they didn't shoot Day. Let them run – I need you in here with Simms.

'On my way, sir.'

'Right.' Palmer turned to Gheeta. 'I think that's got it all covered. Go and ask Hawkins to take the rest of the restaurant staff to the local nick and formally interview them once Simms and Lewis have finished.'

Gheeta nodded and pointed to the tape barrier where a man with a briefcase was being let through. 'Looks like the doctor's arrived, sir – that means a Path van's on its way.'

'Who ordered that?'

'Hawkins.'

'Damn.' Palmer wanted Frome to get a look at Day's body in situ before the doctor did any examination or moved any clothing, but the law states that a doctor must pronounce a person dead before that person can be touched or moved by the Pathology people or morgue van.

'Okay, let the doctor in, but the body stays where it is until Frome's had a look – and get that laptop into an evidence bag. I want Frome to dust it for prints and DNA as a matter of urgency, and then get it back to you to have a look at.'

****

Black and Houseman had sat for a while in their parked car when they arrived back at the scene, looking at the back of the large crowd that was gathering outside the crime tape barrier.

'What the fuck's going on, Trev? You reckon the old bill has raided Day?'

'No, that's not a raid – look, ambulance, loads of plain-clothed and TSG. No, something's gone down heavy. Only one way to find out – come on.'

They left the car and walked to the back of the crowd, not noticing DS Lewis leave her car fifty metres behind them and make her way to the tape where she showed her ID card and was let through. Black asked people what was happening.

'Been a shooting in the restaurant.'

'Somebody said it was an armed police raid.'

'Probably drugs.'

'They reckon the Chinese bloke that owned it is dead.'

'I heard a lady say loads of people were shot, lots dead.'

'Wouldn't be surprised with that place, always looked dodgy to me.'

'Did a good sweet and sour chicken takeaway.'

Black nodded to Houseman and they walked slowly back towards their car.

'She's a clever bitch, that Sammy, a fucking clever bitch.' Houseman was worried. 'Dips my gun, shoots Day with it, and then I bet she left it there so I'm in the frame.'

'With your fingerprints all over it,' Black added. 'And I bet she left that fucking hard drive there for the police as well.'

'I don't give a toss about that, I just want that gun. They'll match the bullet to other hits we've done, and the prints will put my name on them all.'

'And what about the hard drive, Jerry? Day put everything on that laptop – every deal he ever done, every payment he made to the cops, and probably every hit and payment he gave us. That could burn us alive, that fucking hard drive .

****

Sammy had stood in front of Day's desk as he slumped sideways and pitched over onto the floor, taking his chair with him. She turned and waved the gun at Azaff who stood transfixed with fear, it had all been so fast his brain was struggling to catch up and understand what had just happened. Sammy nodded towards the door to the restaurant.

'Go.'

Azaff went.

Sammy put the gun in her pocket and followed him out of the office, mixing into the chaos and pandemonium in the restaurant as customers pushed each other out of the way to get through the single exit door to the street. She saw Azaff go through the swing door marked Private behind the counter that probably led to the kitchens and thought about following him, but she'd stand out; no, stick to the plan and go out with the crowd, and then she could merge into the background and wait and watch.

It was a good half hour that she stood in a shop doorway along the street and watched as the police arrived in numbers and secured the scene; other plainclothes officers arrived and pushed the crowd back and strung crime tape across the road. '*Perhaps the men weren't going to come back? They must have noticed the gun missing by now? Surely they'd retrace their steps to look for it?*'

She was about to move away from the scene when she saw them. They were getting out of the Lexus further away on the other side of the road and walking towards the tape. She made out to be window shopping with her back towards them across the road as they passed. Reflected in the shop window she saw a young lady leave her car further down the road and make her way slowly behind the men. Something wasn't right; why would that lady sit in her car and not hurry to see what was going on behind the tape? It didn't make sense. The only thing that made sense about the lady was the earpiece with a wire that disappeared into her jacket, a wire that wasn't connected to a phone. SHIT! Plainclothes were following the men already.

Sammy watched as the lady went to the end of the tape and was let through; she was definitely police, must have shown an ID. The men had pushed their way to the front in the middle and were in conversation with an officer. Sammy had something important to do. She hurried across the road to the kerbside of the

Lexus and, stooping as though to tie a shoelace, she slipped the gun down into the gutter where anybody opening the passenger door would be bound to see it before she walked away from the scene.

****

'I'm out of here.' Houseman was getting more and more worried as he and Black walked back to the car. 'I'll get a flight to Ireland, I know people there in the Provos who will give me a place for a few days and get a new identity fixed up – new name, papers and passport, and then who knows? Eastern Europe maybe, I've some contacts there.'

Black tried to calm him down. 'Give it a couple of days – get into a hotel and keep your head down, see what happens.'

'You know what's going to happen, I'll get a knock at the door at five in the morning, or more than likely than not the ARU will just smash the door down. FUCK!' He stood on the pavement holding the passenger door open. 'FUCK!'

Black slid into the driver's seat and looked across. 'What? What's up now?'

'The gun, the fucking gun!' Houseman stooped and picked up the gun from the gutter and showed it to Black. 'It was in the gutter.'

'What?'

'Laying there in the gutter, look.' He got in and closed the car door. 'Just fucking laying there.'

Black shook his head in disbelief. 'You fucking idiot – nobody stole it from you. That Samantha girl never dipped you in the restaurant, it must have slipped out of the shoulder holster when you got in the car and wedged between the seat and the door. When you got out just now it fell in the gutter. Fucking hell, Jerry – all that panic for nothing. Get a fucking press stud holster, you dickhead.'

Jerry Houseman relaxed and gave a long sigh of relief. If Jerry Houseman had checked the magazine and found two bullets short, he would not have been so relieved. But he didn't.

****

'Azaff, this is Detective Chief Superintendent Palmer, Serial Murder Squad.' Knight pulled Azaff roughly in front of Palmer. 'Detective

Chief Superintendent Palmer, this is Azaff, lowlife thief and drug pusher.'

Knight had handcuffed Azaff. Azaff didn't like that.

'You've no right to keep me here or cuff me, I haven't done anything. I want a solicitor.'

'Really?' Palmer gave Azaff a cold stare. 'If you haven't done anything, why would you need a solicitor?'

'This is harassment.'

Palmer ignored him. 'What happened in the restaurant? Who shot Mr Day?'

'I was in the kitchen, I didn't see it.'

'No, you weren't – the other staff say you were in with Day when it happened.' Knight moved close to Azaff. 'Perhaps *you* killed him?'

'I don't know, I never saw anything.'

Knight pulled the handcuffs holding Azaff's hands behind his back upwards.

'Ouch!'

'Who shot him?'

'I never saw it.'

'I'll ask you one more time, and then you might have an unfortunate accident trying to run off. You might get a broken nose.'

'What?' Azaff looked at Palmer. 'Did you hear that? He threatened to break my nose!'

128

Palmer knew exactly what Knight was doing and played his part, waving an admonishing figure at Knight. 'Now, now, Knight, we can't go around breaking people's noses just because they won't tell us the truth.' He patted Azaff on the shoulder and gave him a false smile. 'Now then, lad, who shot Mr Day?'

'I told you, I never saw it'

'Break his nose.' Palmer turned and walked off as Knight pushed Azaff against a wall and raised his fist.

'All right, all right!' Azaff shied away from Knight, who was moving close. 'Some girl, she come into the office and shot him twice. I never saw her before, honest.'

Palmer turned back. '*Some girl*? That's hardly a good description, is it?'

'Young, about twenty, blue hair, slim.'

Palmer turned to Knight. 'You think he's telling the truth?'

'No, probably not the whole truth, I think a broken nose would help his memory.'

'It's something to do with the laptop,' Azaff added quickly.

'What laptop?' Palmer feigned ignorance. 'What's a laptop got to do with it?'

'Mr Day had his laptop stolen – got all his cash backhanders to you lot listed on it, all

129

his deals and other stuff. Couple of his men got it back from somebody called Gooch, but the hard drive was missing. They said it had to be some girl called Samantha and went out to find her. Day was having a right go at me for not backing up his files, but all I did was show him how to use it when he got it – he never asked about backing up files or anything. Then this girl comes in and shoots him. I thought she was going to do me too, but she told me to go. You can check it out on the CCTV in the restaurant – and that's it, that's the truth. I swear it.'

'Okay.' Palmer nodded to Knight. 'Take the cuffs off and hand him over to Hamp's men to get a full statement. Then get the CCTV file, sergeant Singh will be able to copy it.'

The CSI van arrived and Reg Frome walked over.

'You're keeping me busy, Justin. What's going on here then?'

'Hello, Reg, been waiting for you. It's all to do with the three murdered lads in the cemetery – seems there's a connection between them and the chap who owned this place, now deceased. There's a laptop in there somewhere that could hold the key, so give it priority if you would – and I gave orders that the body was not to be moved until you'd had a look. I want a ballistics report on the bullets as soon as, please. With a bit of luck, once you've finished we can hand the scene back to the local force to lock down and finish for the day. Steak and kidney pie for dinner tonight, Reg, and Mrs P.'s steak and kidney pie is a real treat not to be missed.' He gave Frome a big smile. 'One of life's pleasures.' He checked his watch. 'It will be cooking in the oven as we speak – the perfect end to an imperfect day.'

DS Singh hurried across to them, her mobile held to her ear. She nodded *hello* to Frome as she listened.

'Once CSI have moved inside, Sergeant, you can hand OIC to Hamp's chap and we can call it a day,' said Palmer, the image of Mrs P.'s steak and kidney pie uppermost in his mind.

Gheeta put the mobile into her tunic pocket. 'Not quite, guv. Gooch has been murdered.'

****

It was close to eleven pm when Palmer finally got home. Henry Gooch's body had been taken to the morgue and his office sealed as a crime scene for Frome's people to comb over in the morning after they finished at Day's. Evening had drawn well into night and the amber street lights of Dulwich Village were a welcome sight. They'd be shut off at midnight as the council strived to manage the government funding cuts. He smiled to himself, thinking of the local lowlife sitting waiting for darkness to cover their nightly search for easy pickings: an open ground floor window, or a car with a catalytic converter parked away from a building. He left the squad car and walked up his drive, making a mental note to cut the front lawn when he got time; hopefully it would be the last cut of the year.

Daisy got a pat as he shut the front door behind him and kicked off his shoes, one of which she walked away with in her mouth. He wasn't going to chase her. Ten years ago he might have done, and would have made it into a game; ten years ago Daisy was a youngster and would have enjoyed it. These days it was more a habit than a game, and she'd drop it somewhere and wander off uninterested.

'Anybody home?' he shouted as he hung his coat and hat on the hallstand.

'In the lounge,' came back Mrs P.'s voice. She was watching a romance on Netflix. 'I'll do you a sandwich in the next break.'

Palmer looked in on her. 'Steak and kidney pie?'

'Benji had it.'

'Benji had it?'

'Steak and kidney won't keep once out of the oven – the crust goes limp soaking up the gravy, you have to eat it straight away. I'll do a sandwich in a minute. I'll make you an individual steak and kidney pie tomorrow.'

'What was Benji doing here?'

'He came to tell me his bitcoin mine is up and running in his shed. It's quite impressive.'

'You had a look?'

'Yes, it's like something from a sci-fi film – all those computers with their red and green lights flashing, very impressive. I rang your mobile to see if you were on your way home, but as usual it was off. So rather than waste the food, Benji sat and had it. I really don't know why you have a mobile phone, it's never on.'

That was very true; Palmer had the comms radio when working and didn't give the mobile a second thought. The only time he'd used it was in the Loot case, and then Gheeta had signalled him to turn it on so she could track where he was on the GPS app she'd installed on it.

The adverts started.

'Come on, you won't like this film – no men kicking a football in it. Cheese or ham?' Mrs P. walked across the hall into the kitchen.

Palmer followed and tripped over the shoe that Daisy had dropped and twisted his ankle.

'Ouch!'

He sat on the floor, rubbing the ankle. Mrs P. poked her head back out of the kitchen.

'What are you doing down there?'

'That bloody dog left one of my shoes on the floor and I tripped on it. I've twisted my ankle and it bloody hurts.'

'You'll live – mind your language. I've told you to leave your shoes in the porch. You want a cup of tea with your sandwich?'

'An anaesthetic would be better.' He held out a hand, expecting help gaining his feet, but he didn't get any as Mrs P. disappeared into the kitchen.

'I'll bring your sandwich and tea into the lounge. You go in, and if the adverts finish tell me what happens in the film.'

'They all die after eating a poisoned steak and kidney pie.'

DAY 6

'You alright, guv?' A worried look set on Gheeta's face as Palmer walked into the Team Room – well, limped not walked.

'Yes, I'm fine – twisted my ankle that's all. Fell over a shoe the damn dog had left on the floor.'

'You should take more care, guv. Broken bones don't set so fast the older you get.' She was hardly able to keep the smile off her face.

Palmer gave her a wilting look. 'Not broken, Sergeant, twisted – like your sense of humour.'

'My gran twisted her ankle.' Claire joined in the conversation from her workstation, giving Gheeta a wink, 'She was never the same after – had to give up the walking football team.'

'I'm not in the walking football team.'

'Have to cross that one off the bucket list then, guv,' said Gheeta with a nod.

'It's not on the bucket list,' Palmer replied.

'Sky diving is out now too,' added Claire.

Palmer held his hands up in surrender. 'Alright, alright, let's get on with the case, shall we?' He threw his coat on a table and sat down. 'Where are the others?'

'Knight's over at Gooch's office talking to the staff in the building, and Lewis and Simms are doubling up on Black and Houseman in case they split up and run,' said Gheeta. 'We've got the comms patched into the speaker.' She nodded to a speaker on the wall. 'Do you want to speak to them, guv?'

'No, no, let them carry on. I want some firm evidence to bring Black and Houseman in.'

'We have got good CCTV, sir,' said Claire. 'Look.'

All three looked at the large plasma screen on the wall as Claire ran the files.

'This is inside the restaurant. Watch the door – here comes Black and Houseman, and Black has a Tesco bag under his arm. They go out of camera shot at the back of the restaurant – maybe going into a back office?'

Palmer agreed. 'Yes, probably to see Day.'

Claire continued. 'Now, if we fast forward ten minutes… There's the queue for the takeaway counter, and coming into view from the bottom now is Black and Houseman – see them?'

'Yes. Whatever business they were doing is over, they haven't got the Tesco bag.'

'And now watch – see the girl coming in from the right? She bumps into Houseman quite hard, lots of apologies, and then Black and Houseman leave. Can't really see if that girl is Samantha Johnson, but I bet it was.'

Gheeta noticed something. 'She got blue hair now – she must have dyed it. Mrs Johnson said it was green.'

Claire carried on. 'I'll run the tape on for ten minutes – nothing happens for that ten minutes.' The tape quickened as the LED corner counter flashed forward until Claire slowed it back to normal speed. 'Then this, watch this – panic in the restaurant. Look, people suddenly rushing for the door, pushing each other out of the way – pure panic. Something is going on that we can't see.'

'They've heard the gunshots from Day's office,' said Palmer.

'And then,' Claire carried on, 'when the place is nearly empty, here she comes again – the girl who bumped into Houseman quickly leaves too.'

The screen went blank.

'So we have Houseman and Black in Day's place just before Day is shot, and both leaving,' said Gheeta. 'Rules them out of the shooting.'

'It's the girl,' said Palmer. 'Got to be Samantha Johnson. She's seen what's on the laptop and who it belongs to and has gone to Day for money, had an argument and shot him.'

'No argument. That Azaff character said she walked in and shot him – no argument, just bang bang you're dead.'

'Why?' Palmer posed the question. 'If she knows what is on the laptop, or more precisely on the hard drive – because let's remember Azaff said the hard drive was missing, and Motörhead said Samantha was a dab hand at computers. So she's had a look and knows what's on it is worth money, but she doesn't go down that route, she just shoots him.' Palmer paused to think. 'Of course!' He got to his feet and quickly sat down again as his ankle sent a shard of pain into his foot. 'Of course she shoots him. She was never after money, she was after revenge – revenge for killing her three friends, so she needed to find out who did it. The laptop was bait – she took out the hard drive as insurance, probably gave it to her mum with instructions to give it to us if anything happened to her, then she put the dud laptop into play to see who came for it.'

'How? How did she put it into play?' asked Gheeta

'Gooch, through Gooch.' Claire was busy on her keyboard changing the file in the screen player. 'Look at this.' She pressed a few keys and the inside foyer of the council offices showed on screen with people milling around. 'This is from the council building where Gooch's office is, and look who comes in – hang on whilst I forward it.' The action sped up and the LED flew round again for a while before she brought it back to normal speed. 'I only got this file half an hour ago so haven't looked right through, but here's a couple we know well coming into the building.'

The screen showed Black and Houseman walking through the foyer.

'And then twenty minutes later…' Claire fast forwarded the action. 'Here they are again leaving. See anything different?'

'One of them is carrying a Tesco bag, the same bag as they had at Day's,' said Palmer, carefully standing and going nearer the screen. 'Right size and shape to have a laptop inside it.'

'Correct.' Claire sat back with a self-congratulatory smile.

'But how did it get there?' asked Gheeta. 'If Samantha Johnson took it to Gooch she should be on the CCTV too.'

Claire nodded. 'Yes, she may be, but I wasn't looking for her – I was looking for Black and Houseman. I'll go back to the start of the day and have another look, now I know what to look for, and see if she makes an appearance earlier.'

'You're looking for a girl going in with a Tesco bag and leaving without one.' Palmer sat back down. 'But did *she* kill Gooch and leave the bag and laptop there, knowing somebody would come and collect it and lead her to Day?'

'She could have, guv,' Gheeta said. 'But only after she was positive somebody was coming to collect it. To know that she must have been there with Gooch when and if he made a call to Day saying he'd got it, and Gooch must have told her Day was sending somebody to collect it. Or she knows Gooch is dodgy like Knight said and left it with him thinking he'd take it straight to Day himself and she'd follow him.'

'I wouldn't have thought she was the kind to be carrying a gun – petty thieves don't get into that scenario. No, I don't think she killed Gooch.'

'What about Day?' Gheeta asked. 'Azaff said she had a gun and shot Day, so she does have a gun.'

'Yes, and I think I know where she got it. If she'd followed Black and Houseman to Day's place you'd think she would stay in the background, not come face to face with the two hoods who are after her. I'll put money on the bullets taken from Day being from one of the guns and matching the ballistics reports on the Red Cross killings Knight showed us. She knows that Black and Houseman would only have the same picture of her we have – younger and with long hair – so an older girl with short blue hair accidently bumping into them in a busy takeaway queue wouldn't raise any concerns.'

'She dipped Houseman.' Gheeta realised where Palmer was going. 'She lifted Houseman's gun and used it to kill Day.'

Palmer nodded. 'Yes, it's brilliant, isn't it? Houseman will get the blame as the bullets will match those from the Red Cross killings.' He took a deep breath. 'Bloody brilliant. We are dealing with a young lady who is very clever.'

'Except for one thing, guv – she's got to get that gun back into Houseman's hands, he must realise it's missing. What's she going to do? Can't just pop it through his letterbox.'

'I don't know, but if the sequence of events we've put together so far is right then she must have an exit plan that gets that gun back to him somehow without raising an alarm.'

Gheeta walked to the progress white board, took the top off the black felt tip and added 'gun' to it with arrows tracing Palmer's theory of the weapon's movement from Houseman to the restaurant to Samantha Johnson to Day and back to Houseman. She put a question mark on the last leg.

Knight came on the speaker. 'Knight to base'

Claire answered. 'Come in, Knight.'

'Nothing at Gooch's office. CSI have finished and I've had a good look, but no hard drive here. Interesting looking at his case files though – quite a few of his clients have crossed my path as re-offenders. Looks like he set them up with drug gangs and other dodgy employment places when they were put on probation with him. We knew he wasn't straight, but seems he was running an employment agency. What do you want me to do now? Over.'

Claire looked to Palmer.

'Come back in.'

Claire conveyed the instruction.

****

'I've got a tail.' Houseman was on his mobile to Black. 'I put the bins out a couple of hours ago and noticed her – single female sitting in a car four doors down. She was still there an hour ago, so I went out and round the corner to the mini-market for some fags and back again, and she was there behind me all the way. She's still there, back in the car now.'

'Okay, hang on a minute. I'll take a look outside here.' Black put his mobile down and walked out of the double doors onto his balcony and made a point of stretching his arms above his head as though he'd just woken up, which wasn't far from the truth. He looked down and along the street; it was single lane each way, and yellow lines on both sides. Simms's solitary parked Nissan stood out. Black went back in and picked up the mobile. 'Yes, I've got company too. We must be in the frame for something.'

143

'Probably the three lads – Johnson's mother could have ID'd us from mugshots.' Houseman was worried.

'Or that fucking Azaff has dropped us in it – they wouldn't be watching us if they weren't close to getting an arrest. Time to disappear,'

'Where?'

'Your Provo mates in Ireland. Can they handle two of us, new IDs, et cetera?'

'Don't see why not.'

'What about your missus? She won't be happy.'

'She'll be very happy – all the money is in her name in case I ever get landed with a Proceeds of Crime order.'

Black laughed. 'Right, pack a bag and come over here. Park on the street and come in the front – my motor's in the underground car park, Ill meet you there, there's a back exit we can use. I'll book the flight. Bring a couple of fake passports – we can't use the proper ones, they'll have our names with Border Control in no time.' He opened his mobile and then had second thoughts; his mobile number would be on Gooch and Days' mobiles, so the police probably had a trace on it and any number he used it to ring would be traced too. He'd better dump that phone when he could. He lifted the receiver on his landline and made the call to Aer Lingus.

'Lewis to base.'

'Come in, Lewis,' Claire answered the call.

'Houseman is on the move. He's driving and he has a large sports bag with him, out'

Palmer took the mic. 'Stay with him, Lewis, keep us up to date. Base out.'

'Will do. Lewis out.'

Palmer walked to the white progress board and thought for a minute before making up his mind. He turned to Gheeta. 'Get a fast car and go over to Southwark County Court, see Judge Laughton and pick up an arrest warrant for both Houseman and Black. I'll get on the phone to him now and arrange for it to be ready. I think it best to pull the pair in now. Large sports bag could be him about to do a runner. I'll tell the judge I consider them both flight risks and they are my principal suspects in a multiple murder investigation so a warrant won't be a problem.'

Gheeta grabbed her coat and was gone as Claire lifted the landline phone and asked the switchboard to be put through to the judge's court office. Laughton was an old friend of Palmer and would write the warrant straight away, unlike some of the newer politically correct breed of judges who would want Palmer to channel the request through AC Bateman and jump through hoops before signing.

Knight came into the office.

'Ah, just the man.' Palmer picked up the mugshots of Black and Houseman from a desk. 'These two, I think it's time to bring them in so I've got a warrant coming. You know them, do I need a ARV with us when we do the arrest? Are they likely to resist?'

'Definitely,' Knight laughed. 'You saw the Red Crosses where we know they have been involved in killings. If they think they're likely to be shaken down for those they'll get nasty, no doubt about it. People like Black and Houseman who make witnesses change their stories, and who other hard men stay clear of, are not going to raise their hands and say '*it's a fair cop, governor*'. They know that if we are going in to arrest them we must have hard evidence, and that means they'll get life.'

'Point taken.' Palmer knew he'd have to get authorisation to deploy an ARV from Bateman; shouldn't be a problem, Bateman had shown how important it was to close this case. Really the correct procedure was that the evidence should all be written up and sent to the CPS for a go-ahead, but that could take weeks to come back from them; no, Palmer needed to act fast before more bodies appeared. If Day's laptop hard drive had the information on it they thought it might have, then others in the criminal world would want to get hold of it and destroy it too. Day would have had dealings over a number of years with most of the major players, and now they'd be worried.

****

'It should go through the CPS, Palmer, you know that.' Bateman was taking a '*by the book*' approach to his request for an ARV team.

'I have a warrant, sir, so I can go in without them – but my information on the suspects is that they won't come quietly.'

147

'The element of surprise, Palmer, use the element of surprise.'

'You don't surprise people like these two, sir. We've got a string of murders we can hit them with and they know it, they'll be on their guard 24/7.'

'It's all circumstantial, Palmer, no hard evidence...'The internal phone on Bateman's desk rang, and he answered it. 'It's for you, your clerk.' He handed Palmer the phone.

'Hello Claire...' Palmer listened for a minute or two. 'Right, that's good. Thank you, Claire.' He handed the phone back to Bateman. 'Reg Frome had the bullets from Day and Gooch's bodies sent down to Ballistics on a fast return request. Both were killed by 9mm bullets from the same gun as used in three of the Red Cross murders. We have CCTV of Black and Houseman going into Gooch's office building and leaving with a package that resembled a laptop, and we have CCTV of the pair of them in Day's restaurant the day he was killed.' He left out the fact that Black and Houseman left the restaurant some time before Day was shot. 'Claire has also just told me that historic ANPR puts their car at or near every one of the Red

Cross killings a day before or on the actual day of those killings.'

Bateman took a deep breath Palmer had him in a corner on this one. 'Alright, I'll arrange an ARV, Palmer – but please try to bring them in without any more deaths, and I want a full report of what we have just discussed with a map of the Red Cross murders and digital copies of the relevant CCTV and ANPR. I have a feeling the CPS might be hammering at the door asking why I bypassed them. Go.'

'Thank you, sir.' Palmer turned and walked to the door.

'Are you limping, Palmer?' Bateman had noticed.

'It's nothing, sir – just twisted my ankle.'

'You should be more careful at your age, Palmer.' One up to Bateman. 'Two year waiting list for a new knee – five years for a hip, you know.' Two up.

'It's a twisted ankle sir, not a busted hip.'

'Yes, but if you are getting a bit unsteady on your feet you never know, do you?' Three up.

'I am not getting unsteady on my feet, sir. I tripped over something.'

149

'Better get your eyesight checked then.' Four up, and a distinct smile on Bateman's face. 'I'll have the ARV paperwork sent down to Firearms.'

****

Samantha Johnson was sat at the kitchen table at her sister's. She rang Motörhead on Cathy's mobile.

'Where are you?' Motörhead asked. 'You okay?'

'I'm fine, I'm at Cathy's. If anybody asks, you don't know where I am.'

'Okay. Those two bastards came back and barged in and took your school picture, and the police had already taken a copy.'

'That's okay, I don't look anything like that now.'

'What's happening, Sammy? Why are you on the run? What have you done?'

'I haven't done anything, mum. I know who killed the Lanes and they know I know, so they are after me – or they were after me, I'm not sure if they still are. It's all a bit involved – but don't worry, the police will be after them so they'll be more worried about that than chasing me.'

'Are you coming home?'

'No, not yet. I'll stay at Cathy's. Don't ring me.'

'Why not?'

'The police will have your phone number and can trace the call. They haven't got mine.'

'Okay.'

'I'll ring you tomorrow.'

'Right-o.'

Samantha finished the call and went back to what she was doing – loading the Day hard drive onto another laptop with an external USB.

Cathy came in from picking up the children from school. 'Right, that's those two settled in front of the telly for a while. What are you doing?'

'Getting rich.'

Cathy laughed. 'Count me in then.'

'I have. The bloke who owned that laptop that the Lanes were killed for wouldn't pay to get it back, so I'm taking a reward.'

'He won't like that.'

'He won't know, he's dead.'

Cathy stood in shocked silence for a while. 'What are you getting into, Sammy? That policeman, Palmer, said I was to ask you to get in contact – maybe you should.'

Samantha noticed the concern in her sister's voice. 'All in good time, don't worry – it's all under control. How would you like your own place?' She gave Cathy a big smile.

****

'Lewis to base.'

'Come in, Lewis.' Claire took the call as Palmer came back into the Team Room from his meeting with Bateman.

'Houseman has pulled up a hundred metres from Black's apartment block at Nine Elms and left his car, taking the sports bag with him, and is walking towards the block.'

Palmer took the mic. 'Simms, have you got eyes on them? Palmer out.'

'Yes, he's entering the slope into the underground car park. Simms out'

'Lewis to base, I'll follow him in. You may lose radio contact whilst I'm in there. Lewis out.'

Palmer turned to Knight. 'What do you think, keep her out?'

152

Knight nodded. 'I would – I wouldn't want her out of contact with those two around.'

'Palmer to Lewis, abort that – walk past and observe from a distance. Repeat, abort, do not go into the car park. Palmer out.'

Silence.

'Palmer to Lewis, did you copy that message? Palmer out.'

Silence.

'Simms to base, Lewis has gone into the car park. Simms out.'

'Palmer to Simms, sit where you are, Simms – advise of any movement, especially Black's car, you've got the registration. Wait for the ARV. Palmer out.'

'Simms to base, will do. Simms out.'

Palmer turned to Knight. 'Get onto Firearms and get the nearest ARV to patch into Simms and liaise with him. Bateman's putting the paperwork through.'

****

'What the fuck!'

Trevor Black came out of the stairwell leading from the apartments down to the resident's car park with a packed suitcase and didn't like what he saw. Houseman stood at the back of the Lexus with a female on her knees next to him with his gun pointing at the back of her head.

'The bitch followed me here, look.' He held up Lewis's radio. 'Policewoman, like we thought. We've got a hostage.'

'We have not – if we take her hostage they'll bring the whole fucking packet after us, we'd have no chance. Bloody hell, Jerry, you idiot.' He threw his suitcase into the back of the car.

'So what do we do then, leave her?'

'Yes.' Black took Houseman's gun and slammed it into the back of Lewis's head. She keeled forward, unconscious. Black slapped her face to make sure she wasn't faking it. She wasn't. He grabbed her under the arms. 'Get her feet and we'll dump her in the corner behind the other cars. Come on.'

They put Lewis as far into the gloom of the rear corner of the car park as they could.

'What about tying her up?' Houseman asked.

Black was in a hurry. 'We haven't time for that – I'd have to go and get a rope. Get in the motor and let's get away. They'll be expecting her to call in and when she doesn't they'll be all over this place. Come on, shove

154

your bag in the boot.' He got in the car and started the engine; Houseman put his sports bag in the boot and jumped into the passenger seat. Black pressed a button on his key fob and the resident's rear exit roller shutter rolled up. He eased the car out of the car park and, carefully observing the speed limit, they left the area.

****

'Palmer to Lewis – come in, Lewis.'

No reply.

'Simms to base, shall I go in?'

'Palmer to Simms – no, wait for the ARV to arrive, these two are armed. We're getting you patched through to the nearest ARV.'

'Understood. Simms out.'

Palmer gave the mic back to Claire. 'Right – come on, Knight, we'd better get over to Nine Elms.'

'Singh to base.'

'Come in, Singh,' Claire answered.

'I have the arrest warrants, I can get to Nine Elms in ten minutes from here. Singh out.'

Palmer had heard and nodded 'yes' to Claire from the doorway before he and Knight left.

155

'That's affirmative, Singh. Palmer and Knight are on their way,' Claire said, adding, 'Take care.'

'I will. Singh out.'

****

'Who said crime doesn't pay?'

Palmer and Knight got out of the squad car and the driver parked it behind the blacked-out ARV minibus in front of Black's apartment block. Palmer looked up at the apartment balconies. 'Very nice too – view of the Thames, serviced apartment, car park. I think Trevor Black is doing quite well out of crime.'

'I don't think the view from a prison cell will be quite the same, sir.' Knight smiled.

They joined Simms and Gheeta.

'Anything happening, Simms?' asked Palmer.

'Nothing, sir – and no contact with Lewis.'

The ARO in charge joined them. He was in full combat fatigues and carrying a carbine. Palmer couldn't see his face behind the reflective helmet visor but saw his embroidered name tag was Bookman. They exchanged greetings.

'What's the situation?' Bookman asked. 'Comms said you think it might be a hostage situation?'

'Yes,' Palmer explained. 'We have one plainclothes female officer in there somewhere and two nasty criminals known to be armed for whom we have arrest warrants.'

'What floor are they on?' asked Bookman.

Palmer looked at Knight.

'Fourth floor, apartment 7.'

Bookman nodded and waved his men out of the minibus. Four moved off to secure the front of the building and make their way to apartment 7; the other four moved in line along the wall of the block and turned into the car park slope, weapons raised.

'It's a dead spot for comms inside there,' Simms made the point.

Bookman called his lead. 'One zero to one four, do you read me?'

'One four, loud and clear.'

Bookman looked at Simms. 'No problem with comms.'

Palmer used his radio. 'Palmer to Lewis – come in, Lewis.'

Nothing.

'She may have turned it off, sir?' said Simms.

'Or maybe somebody else turned it off,' said Gheeta, giving Palmer a worried look.

'One four to one zero.'

'One zero – go ahead, one four.'

'One four, we have one female body in view. Investigating.'

Palmer's heart stopped and fear washed over him. Knight, Simms and Gheeta were transfixed in silence and worry.

'One four, female alive but unconscious. No firearm wounds, blood from head impact wound – request medical assistance, repeat, request medical assistance.'

Palmer acted quickly. 'Palmer to base.'

'Come in, Palmer,' Claire answered.

'Ambulance to Nine Elms, Claire – priority.'

Claire knew better than to ask questions. 'On it now, sir.' She clicked off the comms and hurried over to the internal phone and pressed the red button, which got an immediate response from the call handler department who would despatch the ambulance.

Palmer and the others hurried down the slope into the carpark to where the ARO medic – there's one in every team with an emergency medical pack – was applying a dressing and bandage to Lewis's head. She was now conscious and had been sat up and given an injection to raise her blood pressure. She saw Palmer and the others.

'They clocked me, sir. Sorry.'

'No problem, Lewis. There's an ambulance on its way, get you checked over.'

'I'm fine – a bit dizzy, but fine.'

The medic smiled reassuringly. 'That's your blood pressure being a bit low – often happens after an accident or bump on the head, just nature's way of stemming any blood loss from a wound. Be back to normal in a minute.'

Bookman walked over. 'Apartment 7 is empty, sir – nobody home. Had to break the lock to get in, so I'll arrange a contractor to sort that out. I've left a man on the door.'

'Thank you, Bookman.' Palmer turned to Knight. 'You go and take a look, see if the missing hard drive is up there and give the local station a call and arrange a uniformed officer to take over from the ARO.'

Knight nodded and went off.

The radio crackled into life.

'Base to Palmer.'

159

'Go ahead, Claire.'

'ANPR has picked up Black's Lexus on the move, sir, heading through the West End.'

Palmer looked at Gheeta and Simms. 'Where are they off to then?'

'I'd have thought they'd be heading out of London, not into it,' said Simms.

'Palmer to Base, keep us informed of the route please, Claire. Palmer out.'

'Will do. Base out.'

'Do you need us to stay around, sir?' Bookman was not sure his team were needed anymore.

'No, no, thank you, Bookman – sorry it wasn't more exciting for you.' Palmer gave a smile.

Bookman returned it. 'Believe it or not, that's the way we prefer it, sir. You wouldn't believe how many bits of paper I have to fill in for every bullet fired. Mind you, I wouldn't have minded the paperwork seeing how your WPC was treated.' Bookman nodded and left with his team.

'Base to Palmer.'

'Go ahead, Claire.'

'Black's vehicle is on the Marylebone Road heading east.'

'Copy that. Palmer out.' He looked at Gheeta. 'Where are they going?'

'Safe house in the East End?'

'Could be, but they're not stupid. Why haven't they dumped the Lexus? Black must know we have the number and can follow him on ANPR.'

'Perhaps he and Houseman aren't in it, guv? They could be in another car going in the complete opposite direction using his Lexus as a decoy?'

'Indeed they could, Sergeant, indeed they could.' He clicked on his radio. 'Palmer to base.'

Claire answered. 'Come in, sir.'

'Claire, send the mugshots of Black and Houseman out to all UK Border Force points of exit – airports, passenger docks, et cetera – and put a hold and detain order on them will you please? Palmer out.'

'Will do. Base out.'

'We will be returning to base now, Claire. Palmer out.'

'Copy that. Base out.'

****

'Right, let's go.' Black pulled the handbrake on and turned off the engine. 'Get your bag.' He pushed the button to open the boot.

Houseman was confused as he got out. 'What are we doing here, at St Pancras Station? I thought we were going to Ireland, not France?'

'We are, come on.' Black pulled his suitcase from the back seat as Houseman opened the boot and lifted out his bag. Houseman pointed to the big St Pancras sign. 'Eurostar goes to France, not Ireland.'

'We aren't going on Eurostar, but Palmer will think we are when they find the car here, won't he.' He tapped his head. 'Gotta stay one step ahead, Jerry.' He went to the ticket machine, paid for a ticket and slipped it onto the dashboard in full view. 'Come on.'

They left the car park and hailed a taxi.

'Heathrow please, driver.' Black opened the passenger door for Houseman, who gave him a big smile as they settled in the back of the cab.

'You fucking genius.'

****

'Base to Palmer.'

162

'Come in, Claire.'

'Black's car has been stationary for ten minutes, sir – it's at St Pancras Station, Judd Street car park.'

Palmer looked at Knight and Gheeta.

'Eurostar,' Gheeta said. 'They're heading for France.'

'St Pancras station, driver,' Palmer instructed the driver. 'Fast as you can – put the blues on.' He opened his radio. 'Simms, where are you?'

'Three cars behind you, sir.'

'Okay, you heard that – follow us to St Pancras, blues on. Palmer out.'

'Will do, sir. Simms out.'

Gheeta had opened her laptop and was studying webpages.

'One left for Paris five minutes ago, guv.' She tapped in a number on her mobile. 'I'll see if I can check the passenger list.'

She spoke to the station, giving her name and number, and waited. Palmer was getting agitated.

'What are they doing, tea break?'

'Checking me out with personnel at the Yard, guv – they can't just give out information on passengers without checking that I'm kosher. Data protection.'

'Pity they don't check their passengers' backgrounds just as thoroughly.' Palmer had no time for the nanny state.

St Pancras bookings came back to Gheeta as they raced through the London traffic. She listened and thanked them before turning the mobile off.

'No passengers named Black or Houseman, guv, but they have CCTV of passengers going through the gate to the train if we want it. Have to put an official request through for it - data protection.' A smile lingered on her lips.

'They'll use false names, false passports – they've probably got a bunch of them. How long does the train take to Paris?'

Gheeta checked her laptop. 'Two hours fifteen minutes.'

'Damn, too quick – I was thinking of getting Claire to contact the Paris Embassy and send the mugshots over and see if they couldn't get somebody to check the passengers getting off, just to be sure our targets were on the train. Not enough time – looks like we shall have to be satisfied with an international arrest warrant.'

Twenty minutes later they pulled into the Judd Street car park with Simms behind them and shut off the blues.

'Black Lexus, BLK1,' said Knight, scanning the cars. 'I know that off by heart.'

'Don't tell me, Houseman's is HM1?' Palmer said. 'Arrogant pair.'

'It's JER1,' said Knight.

'There it is.' Gheeta pointed at the Lexus parked against the wall on the ground floor.

They walked over to it.

'They even paid for a ticket.' Knight leant to read the ticket on the dashboard through the windscreen. 'Two hours, fifteen quid.'

'How much?' Palmer couldn't believe the price.

'Fifteen quid.'

'When was it bought, what time?' asked Palmer.

'Thirty five minutes ago.'

'Why two hours, guv?' asked Gheeta. 'Why even bother with a ticket?'

'I don't know.' Palmer looked round the car. 'Could be they didn't come here to get the train and are coming back to the car?'

'Doesn't make sense.' Knight shook his head. 'Black's no fool, he knows we have his car number and he also knows after the episode at his apartment building that we are after him and we'd be all over it on ANPR. So I can't see him parking and then wandering back in two hours, knowing we would have found it and be waiting. No, he's up to something.'

Palmer nodded. 'Okay, but we have no alternative but to park up and watch for an hour and a half until the ticket runs out, do we? Just in case they do come back.'

The radio crackled as Claire called.

'Base to Palmer.'

Palmer answered. 'Go ahead, base.'

'I have Mr Frome here, he would like a word, sir. Base out.'

'Put him on, Claire. Palmer out.'

Reg Frome came on the line. 'Justin, I thought you'd like to know we gave the Black apartment a quick once-over and didn't find anything of interest. But he's got a normal BT landline and when we were dusting it for prints I thought to press the redial button, and guess who answered? Frome out.'

'Who? Palmer out.'

'Aer Lingus booking office, Heathrow. Frome out.'

Palmer looked at his team. 'This bloody car is a decoy, they never intended to take the Eurostar – probably got somebody else to drive it here, knowing we'd follow it whilst they went to Heathrow and off to Ireland.'

Palmer went back to the radio. 'Thanks, Reg – put Claire back on please. Palmer out.'

'She's on the external phone, she's checking the Aer Lingus passenger manifest with Border Control. Frome out.'

'I hope they're quicker than British Rail Eurostar.' Palmer covered the radio and made the remark to his team.

'She's going through Border Control, guv,' Gheeta said. 'They'll do it in minutes.'

'I don't think they'll find anything – our targets will be using false passports.' Palmer didn't hold much hope of a definite hit.

He was right, Claire came back with a negative; no Black or Houseman was listed as a passenger with Aer Lingus that day. The best they could do was email the mugshots to the Airport Police and hope one of them might spot the pair on the concourse. Border Control at Customs already had them.

'Right.' Palmer decided to keep chasing. 'Simms, you park up here and keep an eye on the Lexus – if they do return, call it in and follow. If not, give it a half hour over the parking time and then call for a low-loader and get it taken to the nearest pound and covered. I'll get Frome to have a couple of his people to go over it in case there's anything inside to tie it into any of the Red Cross murders, okay? The rest of us, onward to Heathrow.'

'Yes, fine,' said Simms, disguising his disappointment at being left behind.

****

The taxi was making good time ahead of the rush hour and turned onto Chelsea Bridge.

Black took his gun from his shoulder holster and his mobile from his coat pocket. 'Give me your mobile.'

Houseman gave Black a questioning look in the back of the taxi. 'What, why? What are you doing?'

'Just give it to me.'

He took it from his jacket pocket and handed it over.

'And your gun.'

'My gun?'

'There's no way we'll get our guns through Customs at the airport, is there? Be easy enough to buy a couple in Ireland, I'm sure your Provo mates will oblige.'

Houseman slipped the gun from his shoulder holster and handed it over. Black took a fifty pound note from the bundle in his inside pocket, leant forward and pressed the driver's intercom. 'Stop on the bridge please.'

'Red line guv, it's a clearway I can't.'

'An extra fifty quid on the fare says you can.' Black held the note to the driver's safety screen. The screen lowered and a hand took the note. The screen went back up and the taxi stopped at the side of the road, halfway across the bridge.

Hiding the mobiles and guns under his coat, Black got out, walked to the parapet and leant over it, feigning sickness, and dropped the guns and mobiles into the brown water below, before returning to the cab and nodding to the driver, who pulled the cab out into the traffic and resumed their journey, fifty pounds richer.

****

Palmer's car was speeding along the Westway, blues on, siren blaring, when the call came through.

'Base to Palmer.'

'Go ahead, base. Palmer out.'

'Good news, sir – Black and Houseman have been detained at Heathrow. Sharp-eyed Customs official recognised them, they are travelling on fake passports. Border

Control has them in custody under the arrest warrant and want instructions, Base out.'

The mood of worry in the car turned into jubilation, smiles all round. Knight and Gheeta high fived.

'Palmer to base, inform Bateman please, Claire, and have two plain cars go to the airport and do a transfer from Border Control to the Met and bring them back to the Yard. I want them kept apart from now on please. We will return to base. Palmer out.'

'Copy that. Base out.'

'Simms, did you copy that? Palmer out.'

'I did. Simms out.'

'Okay, put a call in for that low-loader now then, and once the car is in a pound return to base. Palmer out.'

'Will do. Simms out.'

****

'You're in a good mood,' Mrs P. greeted Palmer when he arrived home that evening. He was humming an unrecognisable tune as he hung up his coat and trilby; all the tunes Palmer hummed were unrecognisable. He sat on the bottom stair, changed into his slippers, gave Daisy a pat, checked that she hadn't dropped anything in his path, and wandered into the kitchen.

'I'm always in a good mood,' he responded. 'The epitome of joviality and good moodiness, that's me.' He sat at the table.

'That is definitely NOT you.' Mrs P. served up the individual steak and kidney pie she had cooked for him and sat opposite with a tuna salad. 'You'd better enjoy that, steak will be off the menu soon.'

'Why?'

'Global warming – apparently cows contribute more to global warming than anything else.'

'How?' Palmer was enjoying the meal. 'They don't light fires.'

'Passing wind.'

'Farting?'

Mrs P. closed her eyes. 'Passing wind is the correct term.'

Palmer was on a roll; he knew how Mrs P. hated it when he reverted to common language and continued to bate her.

'Business opportunity there – cow corks, corks you can stick up a cow's...'

She stepped in. 'Yes, that's quite enough about that, thank you, Justin. Eat your pie.

171

'Could make millions – by the way, talking about business opportunities how's our neighbour doing with his bitcoin mine, made a million yet, has he?' There was a sarcastic edge to Palmer's question.

'He popped in earlier, said it's all working and going well. He's got a new lawnmower now as well, one of those robotic ones – said we could borrow it.'

'A what?'

'Robotic lawn mower. You know, you've seen them on telly – round disc things that keep mowing the lawn automatically by sensing the edge and turning round. You can get them for hovering the house as well – anything in their way and they go round it.'

'How do they do the stairs?'

'They don't.'

'Aha! See, technology hits a brick wall – or at least a wooden staircase.'

Mrs P. had to smile. 'You're daft.'

'What's wrong with a normal hover anyway?'

'Nothing, but these robotic things do it automatically. You switch them on and leave them to it.'

'The way things are going the human race will have no need of arms and legs in the future. Mind you, from what I see every day a good percentage have already dumped their brains.'

'Eat your pie.'

'It's very tasty – can't beat a bit of British beef.'

'It's a bit of British tofu, actually – plant-based, no meat.' She gave him a wide smile. 'One less fart, eh?'

****

Something was wrong. The sound of sirens was dragging Palmer out of his sleep and Mrs P.'s elbow repetitively digging into his back wasn't helping; nor was Daisy barking downstairs.

'What's going on?' The blue flashing lights lit the bedroom through the curtains. His first thought was that Blake and Houseman had got free and a car had been sent for him, but as his brain clicked into gear he realised he would have been phoned first. He swung himself out of bed and made his way over to the window, pulling the curtain aside as Mrs P. joined him. At the front of the house stood a fire engine, its hose being quickly unrolled up Benji's drive by the fire fighters.

'Benji's on fire!' Mrs P. stated the obvious assumption.

Palmer ran out of the bedroom and along the landing into the bathroom where he opened the frosted glass window which looked out onto Benji's and their back gardens. The house wasn't on fire, but Benji's new shed was – together with a section of Palmer's fence! The shed roof had caved in and flames were shooting up into the night. Palmer went back to the bedroom; the light didn't work when he flipped the switch. He pulled on a pair of trousers and a jumper and slippers before making his way downstairs; none of the lights worked. He navigated to the front door, giving Daisy a pat on the way. 'Good girl, stay there.'

He swapped his slippers for a pair of boots in the porch and hurried into his front garden and through the gate Mrs P. had insisted on having that led from their front garden into Benji's, to save her walking all the way round when she helped with his gardening, which she very often did, much to Palmer's annoyance. He saw the white helmet of the station officer stood near the house with Benji as the fire crew directed the hose to quell the flames and made his way across to them.

The station officer gave him a broad smile. 'Hello, Justin – never a dull moment, eh?'

Palmer knew the station office and most of the fire fighters by name and they knew him. Local emergency services like to keep tabs on each other as their work often overlaps, and although Palmer wasn't based locally he was a great supporter of the local fire service and hospital, and Mrs P. held open days in their garden during the summer to raise money for them, whilst he would make himself available to help on their open days.

Benji was looking a trifle distraught, standing beside the station officer in a Hawaiian tie-dyed bed shirt, hairnet and flip flops. 'I'm so sorry, Justin – I don't know what happened. If there's any damage to your fence, I'll pay.'

Any damage? That section of fence was now a smouldering gap over a pile of wet ash and charcoal.

Palmer wouldn't admit it, but he was quite pleased Benji hadn't tried to douse the fire himself and suffered any burns; it was still quite fierce and they could feel the heat a good twenty yards away.

'What happened, electrical short?'

The station officer shook his head. 'No, apparently Mr Courtney-Smythe says there were about a hundred computers in there going full blast mining bitcoins. Overheated I would think – third one that we've had self-ignite this month. Did you harvest any coins?' he asked Benji.'

'No, it's only been operating for two days.'

'Shame, if you had you could at least cover the cost of Mr Palmer's new fence.'

Palmer looked at the tangled mess of burnt wood and melted computers, 'Better hope scrap metal prices rise.'

'Hey-ho, now you're for it.' The station officer nodded towards the road where a London Electricity van was pulling up. 'They won't be too pleased with you.'

And they weren't. Two grim-faced donkey jacketed operatives made their way up the drive.

'Mr Courtney-Smythe?' asked one as they approached.

'Yes, that's me.' Benji put on a false smile and offered his hand, which was refused.

'London Electric,' said the man in an official tone. 'What have you been doing here?' He looked at what was left of the shed, 'Don't tell me, bitcoin mining?'

'Yes,' Benji answered sheepishly.

'How many linked computers were in there?'

'A hundred.'

'A HUNDRED?'

Palmer thought the London Electric man was going to have a heart attack.

'Yes.'

The man couldn't believe it. 'A hundred computers on a standard domestic electric supply?'

'Yes.'

'To run that many you should have an industrial supply, not a domestic one – no wonder it went up. You've blown out the local sub-station as well – no power between here and Peckham until our crew repair it. The power your computers tried to pull through the system turned your domestic wiring into heater elements like an electric fire – they can't carry that amount and set the cables on fire, and then your shed. You're lucky your house meter didn't go up and set your house on fire too. We could have you arrested for this.'

'Tea, anybody?' Mrs P.'s homely voice cut in as she approached with a tray of tea cups. 'Help yourself to sugar and biscuits. I'll go and get another tray for the men.'

It always amazed Palmer how Mrs P. could appear within twenty minutes of getting out of bed, unruffled in a smart trouser suit, hair done and make-up on. Benji in his tie-dyed Hawaiian bed shirt, hairnet and flip flops should take lessons.

****

DAY 7

There was an air of relief in the Team Room the next morning. Clairc was collating the various bits of information as they came in; in-depth searches inside Black's apartment and Houseman's home were going on, Forensics were swarming over the Lexus, and witnesses to the Red Cross murders were being re-interviewed with the hope that if they knew Black and Houseman were now under arrest for those crimes, they might remember a little more. Knight, supported by Simms, was holding the first interviews with the pair, and no surprise that every question was met with 'no comment'. Gheeta meanwhile made application to the magistrates' court for a maximum ninety-six day custody extension on the pair which, seeing the charge was one of multiple murder, would be granted. Even so, Palmer took no chances and had her apply for it through Judge Laughton at Southwark County Court. Lewis sat at a table and collated all the case paperwork into chronological order.

AC Bateman was their first visitor and offered his congratulations and, seeing how busy they were, he didn't hang about but went up to his office to work out a strategy whereby he could claim a big part, if not all, of the success.

It was still worrying Palmer that the evidence was all circumstantial, they needed definite witnesses or conclusive forensic evidence; the CPS could be very anti if a prosecution was put forward to them on just circumstantial evidence. And there was still Samantha Johnson out and about; what was she up to, and more to the point, if she had the hard drive from the laptop, what was on it that signed a death warrant for three lads, and possibly Gooch and Day as well?

His thoughts were interrupted by Lucy Price coming in. He rolled his eyes, knowing full well why she was there.

'No good looking like that, Justin,' Lucy laughed out loud. 'The natives are restless – press briefing at 11a.m., or there will be lots of false headlines and news reports going out. Just need a holding statement to keep it all in our control.'

Palmer nodded; he understood the reasoning, and it could afford him the opportunity to put the search for Samantha Johnson firmly in the public domain now her probable assassins were in custody.

****

The mugshots of Samantha, Black and Houseman made the first editions of the *Evening Standard* and the midday radio and television news broadcasts. Bateman hadn't attended the press briefing; either Palmer's caustic remark about his help at the last one had hit home or he was busy telling his superiors how he, personally, had engineered the arrests – probably the latter.

Gheeta had returned from the magistrates' court with the signed custody extensions and a celebratory bag of Big Macs for the team. They sat and watched the midday news bulletin as they ate.

The afternoon started with Reg Frome ringing with news that they had found a clip of 9mm bullets in Houseman's garage, the same calibre as those used in some of the Red Cross shootings and also Gooch and Day's killings.

'It's all still circumstantial,' Palmer pointed out to the Team. 'You can't compare new bullets to those that have been fired to get a match. We need the guns.' But at least it was a link, however tenuous.

Claire took a call on the internal phone.

'Have you ordered a cab, sir?' she asked Palmer.

'No, why?'

'There's a taxi driver at the front desk asking for you.'

****

'You think it was about here?' Palmer asked Harry Cohen, London Taxi Driver 21586 as they got out of the plain squad car halfway across Chelsea Bridge.

'I can't be totally sure, but I think it was about here. He went to the edge and did something – I wasn't really watching, I was watching the road. it's a clearway, I didn't want a ticket.'

'Why did you stop, one of them feeling sick?'

Harry Cohen shrugged. 'No, to be honest he offered me fifty quid to stop.'

'He dumped the guns, guv.' Gheeta thought it was obvious. 'You don't pay fifty pounds to be ill. They knew they'd never get them through the Customs metal detectors at Heathrow and couldn't take a chance leaving them anywhere. I'll stake fifty quid they're on the river bed.'

Palmer agreed. 'I think you're right, Sergeant. Get onto the Thames Division and see if we can't get some divers up here. There can only have been a couple of tides since yesterday, so maybe they are still visible on the river bed.'

****

It took a couple of hours to set things up and the evening was drawing in as Palmer, Knight and Gheeta stood on the embankment, watching the divers taking to the Thames from the police launches. Lewis and Simms had been thanked for their help on the case, thanked and released back to their own stations after Bateman had called Palmer and questioned the need to keep them now Black and Houseman were in custody.

'Budgets, Palmer, every penny on overtime comes out of your department's budget. If they are not imperative to the investigation, I'm afraid they must go.'

Much as Palmer would have liked them to stay and see the case through to the end, he really couldn't justify any more expense. Lewis and Simms understood; they'd be first on Gheeta's list next time the call for reinforcements went out.

183

Knight was okay to stay as his OC department was within the same budget as the SMS.

'Anything of interest?' Palmer asked the Thames Division OIC standing beside them on the embankment.

'A couple of knives and a Roman coin so far, sir. The knives could prove interesting – so many postcode gang stabbings these days, no doubt Pathology will be able to match them to a deceased kid's wounds.'

The London drugs problem was basically out of control. Every street corner had a hooded dealer, with a pharmacy in their pockets to satisfy every addict's preference. Palmer had been internally sanctioned for expressing the view at the last DCI conference that perhaps the Home Secretary should turn her attention to that rather than a few hundred migrants coming across the channel each week.

'Bit dark down there now, isn't it?' Palmer asked the OIC, nodding towards the river. 'Can't see much, can they?'

'It's fine, the divers have lights and submersive metal detectors. If we don't get a positive tonight I'll get a magnet sent up tomorrow'

'A magnet?'

The OIC laughed. 'Yes, bit like the ones you see in scrap yards, only not so big. We drag it about a foot above the river bed and it picks up anything metallic. Hang on, we have a call.'

He pointed out to where a diver was head above the water with his arm held up; he was holding a gun.

Palmer turned to Gheeta. 'Good job nobody took your bet, looks like you'd be fifty quid in.'

In the next hour the second gun and the two phones were brought from their watery grave and sent by motorbike to the National Ballistics Intelligence Service and Digital Forensics for analysis.

****

DAY 8

Unusually for him, Palmer was in the Team Room first the next day; he'd driven himself in, beating the rush hour, he was still feeling the pain of the twisted ankle but not so much. He was champing at the bit to get the results back on the guns and mobiles. He knew it wouldn't happen for a few hours but wanted to go through the paperwork on each of the Red Cross killings, as well as some new witness statements the local force detectives had managed to prise out of previously reluctant witnesses now the Black and Houseman threat was nullified by their arrest. Both Black and Houseman had now been identified from mugshots by several witnesses who *hadn't seen anything* in their previous statements, and the Lexus had been put near to the killings on the day before or on the day by historic ANPR. If the ballistics came through with a positive on the bullets matching the retrieved guns, it would be a solid case.

Gheeta, Knight and Claire came in carrying coffees. Greetings were exchanged.

'Saw your car in the car park, guv, so bought you a coffee.' Gheeta placed the mug in front of him. 'Wet the bed, did you?' She gave an obvious look at the wall clock.

'Ha ha,' Palmer gave a false laugh. 'No, I didn't wet the bed – I wanted to get this Red Cross paperwork in order for the CPS with the new witness statements. I can't see they can fail to prosecute now.'

'If the forensics on the guns come through positive they'll have no alternative, guv.' Gheeta took off her coat and switched on the bank of computers as Claire answered the internal wall phone that buzzed loudly.

She put the receiver back on its hook. 'Package for you at the post room, sir.'

'A package?' Palmer screwed up his eyes. 'Not expecting anything, are we?'

Gheeta shook her head. 'Not as far as I know. I'll go and get it.'

She returned fifteen minutes later and put a small brown paper-wrapped package on the table in front of Palmer. All mail to Scotland Yard was taken by the Royal Mail to the secure post room, where it was scanned and checked for explosives, poison, liquids and drugs. No chance was taken on anything nasty getting through.

'It's been scanned and checked for explosives and brushed for prints, none found. It's safe – the scan looked like a small radio.'

'I think we can guess what it is then,' Palmer said as he cut open the package and slid out a thin metal tray with a motherboard sunk into it covered with numerous computer chips and fine wires. 'I take it this is the reclusive hard drive?' He looked at Gheeta.

'Yes, now we can find out what all the fuss is about, guv.' She went over to the store cupboards under the computer desks and searched through two before she found what she was after. 'I knew I had one in here somewhere.'

'One what?' asked Palmer.

'Exterior hard drive adapter.' Gheeta held up a thick cable with a USB plug on one end and a small flat push-in connector that resembled a mobile phone charger connector on the other. 'Right then, let's see what we've got.' She moved to her main computer and carefully pushed in the connector to the small receiving socket on the hard drive and pushed the USB into a socket on the side of her computer keyboard. 'Fingers crossed.'

Gheeta tapped on her keyboard and a file appeared on the screen; she moved the mouse over it and double clicked. The file opened and filled the screen. It was a list of contents and names.

'Whoo! Whoo! No passwords, Houston, we have lift off!' She turned and beamed at Palmer. 'No password, easy peasy.'

Knight leant forward and looked at the screen. 'I know some of these names. Gilchrist, Hanley, Prior, Billingham.'

'Really?' Palmer couldn't place any of them. 'Dealers?'

Knight shook his head. 'No, OC officers – Prior is in my team. Jesus, this information is dynamite if it's what we think it is.'

'Hang on.' Gheeta clicked on Prior and a page opened with PRIOR at the top and underneath a list of dates and payments. 'Doesn't take a genius to work out what all that means, does it?'

'Brown envelopes.' Knight was angry. 'The bastard. No wonder we never found anything at Day's when we raided the restaurant, or his bloody four million pound house. Prior will go down for this, I'll make sure of that – if Commander Long doesn't kill him first!'

'Okay, now listen, and listen carefully all of you,' Palmer was serious. 'This is not our problem and certainly doesn't come under this department's remit. Sergeant, you carry on through the information on that hard drive file by file and see if there is anything in there that relates directly to our current case. That's all I'm interested in, the rest of it will be sent to the relevant departments including Internal Affairs, but through Bateman. Any information found on that hard drive stays within this room – that is an order, understand?'

They nodded yes.

'Knight, you understand?'

'Yes.'

'Good. Carry on then, Sergeant.'

'Yes, guv.'

'Claire, give Digital Forensics and Ballistics a call please – put some pressure on them to get the reports on the phone and bullets through to us pronto.'

'Will do.' Claire stood and took the internal phone book with her to the wall phone to make the calls.

****

It was Day's online bank account details on a file in the hard drive that provided the best information, even to the bank passwords being listed on the first page. Day obviously had no idea about security or hadn't thought that anybody would have the temerity to steal anything belonging to *him*. Once Gheeta had collated all the information the team gathered chairs around her computer desk late in the afternoon and listened as she took them through her findings.

'Right.' She cleared her throat. 'Mr Day was a very wealthy man. Over the last month his banks – notice I say *banks* – received nearly a million pounds in cash. He had sixteen bank accounts spread over ten banks. The cash was split down to amounts that didn't need the banks to raise any suspected money laundering paperwork when he deposited it, although as usual with banks I suspect they knew what was happening. Banks are very reluctant to blow the whistle and lose a client depositing that amount of cash on a regular basis.

'So, the money was split and started off being deposited into five of the sixteen accounts at the banks – then working online, Day, or somebody working for him, would split it again and transfer those splits online to other banks, then repeat the process until the initial amount was spread between most of the sixteen bank accounts. It is then swapped between them, again by online transfers, before the process is then reversed and the money eventually comes back the same way to the initial ten banks, all now laundered and clean. A bank will not question a transfer from another bank as they have the excuse that *'it's coming from a bank so it must have been through the money laundering protocols*. The forensic accountants call this method of money laundering *layering*. Once it was *clean* and back into Day's ten main accounts, he was able to take out large amounts of cash without raising any of those banks' laundering flags – and he did, hundreds of thousands in cash at a time. Probably to pay his narcotic suppliers – cash is king in that business.'

'It's not magic, is it?' Palmer commented. 'Just bloody clever. If Pablo Escobar had thought of it he wouldn't have had to keep his billions in buried oil drums.'

'I've checked with the main banks and there's seven and a half million in Day's main five accounts, plus more in his wife's account'

'If he banked close on a million in the last month, he must have had a lot more than seven and a half million through his hands over the years,' Palmer said, wondering where it was.

192

Knight knew the answer. 'Property, sir – over the years he's bought up half of Canary Wharf, and his money is developing Nine Elms where Black's apartment is. Probably gave it to him in lieu of payment for the Red Cross killings.'

'I think you'd better get all this financial information up to Forensic Accounts and have them put a stop on his and his wife's accounts – if she's party to his financial gymnastics she might move it all overseas,' Palmer told Gheeta. 'I think they might like to issue a Proceeds of Crime order on the cash and property. I don't think Mrs Day will be able to furnish them or HMRC with any accounts showing all those property deals as being financed by legitimate income.'

'I will do, sir. There's a couple of other things too.'

'Go on.'

'Black's name is on the list of people Day made payments to. And the dates of the payments collate to within two or three days after each of the Red Cross murders.'

Palmer smiled. 'Got him – his motor is caught on ANPR at or near the murders on the day or just before, and he gets payments from

Day a few days after. It might be circumstantial, but it's bloody hard circumstantial.'

'And one last abnormality on the money, guv,' Gheeta added.

'Go on?'

'Well, there's a transfer out of one of Day's main accounts of eight hundred thousand pounds.'

'No doubt a large consignment of cocaine arrived.'

'This was taken out after he was dead, guv.'

Palmer thought for a moment. 'The wife? Setting herself up before there's a stop put on the account?' He checked his watch. 'Banks are closed now. Talk to that bank first thing in the morning, no more withdrawals allowed – and also Forensic Accounts, get them to freeze all the accounts.' He stood and stretched his arms. 'Good work today, team. We should get the reports on the bullets and phones tomorrow and have enough to persuade the CPS to file charges.'

****

194

Palmer parked his CRV on his drive and got out. He looked across to where Benji's shed used to stand, now just a gap. The air still had a slightly smoky edge to it. He even felt a little sorry for Benji, not a feeling he often had for his neighbour. He walked up the drive, admiring the large flower bed of asters that Mrs P. had planted last spring to brighten up the front garden in the autumn, which had previously been grass with a rose bed border. The asters were starting to bloom; she'd be pleased.

Inside, the smell wafting down the hall from the kitchen was of moussaka, another of Palmer's favourite meals, always served with a topping of burnt cheese. He had peculiar tastes.

Life was good; the case would be cleared up tomorrow, moussaka for tea, and the football season had started and was on Sky. What could possibly go wrong? He shut the front door, turned and fell over Daisy, who was standing behind him with a slipper in her mouth.

****

DAY 9

'Why don't you get a medic to take a look at that ankle, guv? Your limp seems to be getting worse.' Gheeta was genuinely concerned.

Palmer had called for a car to bring him to the Yard that morning as his ankle had swollen and made pressing the pedals when driving a bit painful. He had exchanged the usual 'good mornings' with Claire, Gheeta and Knight before putting his coat and trilby on a table.

'Nah, it's just the joint aching a bit as the bruise comes out – be fine in a couple of days, nothing to worry about. How did the meeting with the bank go?'

'Very interesting, guv. It seems Mrs Day often visited to withdraw large amounts – Day would email the bank with details of the amount and when she would call. I checked the emails on his hard drive and that's exactly what he did with the last withdrawal too.'

Palmer raised his eyebrows. 'So how did he manage that being dead?'

'Exactly, *he* obviously didn't – and one more thing, it wasn't Mrs Day who collected

196

the money this time. The email supposedly from Day said that as his wife was 'on holiday', his assistant, Miss Lane, would collect it.'

'Samantha Johnson.'

'The lady who collected it was in her twenties and had blue hair and knew the account password so it must have been somebody who had access to the laptop files.'

'Samantha Johnson.'

'She's a clever one, isn't she?' Knight smiled his admiration for Samantha's move. 'And now eight hundred thousand richer.'

'CCTV?' asked Palmer.

'Yes, I had a look,' said Gheeta. 'But you couldn't tell anything from it – trousers and a hoodie, could be male or female, and she kept her face turned away from the cameras. She'd done her homework on the bank cameras.'

'The ballistics report is through.' Claire had walked over to the printer which had started to print out sheets of paper. She collected them from the tray and passed them to Palmer, who took a seat and read through. The others waited with bated breath; it had to finger Black and Houseman, there was no other scenario.

Palmer's smile told them it did; he read out loud from page three of the report. *'At each of the Red Cross killings, the bullets removed from the bodies were fired from either firearm A or firearm B of the two guns recovered from the Thames. In three cases, bullets from both the guns were present.* Bingo! Plus, *Henry Gooch and Robert Day were killed by a single bullet from firearm A. The firearms have been sent onto Reg Frome at Murder Squad Forensics for fingerprint and DNA analysis.'*

'Won't get any fingerprints after being in the water, will they?' Claire asked.

'They might well do.' Knight was hopeful. 'Those guns were only in the water a day or so – it takes a few days for prints to disperse in water.'

'Right, Sergeant, give the CPS a call and arrange a meet. Claire, you add the ballistics report to the case paperwork so we can present the lot to them, and then give the regional squads a 'hurry up' with any new witness statements. I don't think Messrs Black and Houseman will be going home for some time, if at all.'

'What about Day's murder, guv?' Gheeta could see a loose end. 'Bullet from Houseman's gun but neither he nor Black were there, and Lewis was tailing them so that's a rock hard alibi – although they don't need one as

CCTV and Azaff's statement put Samantha Johnson firmly in the frame for that one.'

Palmer had already thought about that. 'Not our problem, Sergeant. Our case is to catch the killer or killers of three young men – we've done that. The murder of Day is not in that remit. I intend to pass that to Organised Crime.' He gave Knight a smile. 'I also intend OC to have Day's hard drive, and for Commander Long to make a decision on Officer Prior. Sometimes it can be useful to know you've a leak in the department, as long as you know who it is. The rest of the names I expect to be given to Bateman, and then it's his and Internal Affairs' problem. Are you okay with that, Knight?'

'Yes, that's fine – going to be difficult not to punch Prior's lights out though.'

'I'm sure you'll manage to control yourself – at least you've caught him. I think you might find it a bit more difficult catching Samantha Johnson.' He gave a shrug. 'Personally I think that young lady has done us and the public a favour.'

****

Palmer and Singh spent most of the afternoon across the corridor in his office talking through the case with the CPS prosecutor; she was happy that they had watertight cases of serial murder to charge Black and Houseman with. An hour into their discussion, Claire interrupted with the digital forensic results on the two phones retrieved from the Thames. She had downloaded the list of calls made and received on each of them for the dates around the Red Cross murders, and on each occasion a call was made on the actual day of the murder from or near to the actual murder location to Robert Day's phone from one or other of Black's or Houseman's mobiles. This tied in nicely with the money sent from Day's account to Black's a day or two after. It was obvious Black had phoned Day after the hit had been carried out and Day had made the payment. That information overlaid on the ANPR record of Black's Lexus, and the jigsaw was complete.

****

Dusk was falling as Palmer got out of the squad car at his house, thanked the driver, shut the door and limped up the drive.

He came to an abrupt halt as his eyes caught sight of something not quite right. The gate between his and Benji's gardens was open; Mrs P. must have been through, probably to help Benji clear up the burnt shed mess. Hopefully Benji had booked somebody to come and replace the fence fairly soon too. He walked over to shut the gate and then noticed the two foot wide mowed section of the grass leading through the gate and down to Mrs P.'s new Aster bed and into it, leaving a trail of mowed and desiccated Asters along it. Benji's robotic mower had obviously escaped through the open gate and was the culprit. He walked to the edge of the Aster bed and peered into the gloom, trying to see where the mower was now when it hit him hard from behind on his dodgy ankle, sending him to the ground.

****

DAY 10

Funerals were not to Palmer's liking. Over his career he'd had to attend quite a few; those involving deceased children and young people were the worst. The Lanes' and Frederick Smith's funerals were booked for eleven in the morning the next day. Palmer decided to go. Nobody deserved to die the way they had, and he felt he ought to pay some respects; even if they were criminals.

Knight helped him out of the squad car at the cemetery. The driver had got as near as he could on the tarmac path but there was still fifty metres across to the grave side.

Palmer held onto Knight's arm as Gheeta in civilian clothes pulled his NHS crutch from the car and Palmer slipped his arm into it. He only needed the one crutch to take the weight of his now broken ankle as he walked.

Mrs P. had called an ambulance the evening before after hearing his calls for help from the drive and finding him laying there in agony. The medics had given him a painkiller and taken him to King's College Hospital, where a broken ankle was confirmed and a sleeve of plaster slapped around it to set it. The good news was the X-ray had shown it to be a clean break, so no complications, and once it had set he'd be back to normal on his feet.

Benji's robotic mower had made its escape and suffered a tragic end when a bus ran over it on the Norwood Road.

'Looks like a good turnout, guv – got to be a hundred plus.' Gheeta looked across at the crowd of mourners gathered around the grave. The ceremony for the Lanes and Fred Smith was well underway.

'Popular lads,' said Palmer, impressed with the numbers. 'Very popular by the look of it.'

They made their way across the grass and stopped twenty metres away.

'That's near enough, I think,' said Palmer. 'Not everybody on the Bevan estate would be happy to see the police here.'

'Have you noticed something, sir?' Knight was looking at the row of mourners.

'What?'

'Look at the ladies' hair.'

Palmer looked and Palmer saw. 'Well, well, well, she's in there somewhere then.'

Every female from middle age down had bright blue hair.

'We can't arrest them all, guv,' said Gheeta. 'Having blue hair isn't an offence.'

'There's no warrant out for Samantha anyway.' Palmer smiled. 'This young lady continues to impress me.'

'... and there's three graves, guv.' Gheeta was surprised. 'I thought it was a council paid burial?'

'As far as I know it is, but I think even the local council would have a job explaining burying three people in one pauper's grave, Sergeant. Even with the government cut-backs.'

Knight hadn't heard of paupers' burials before. 'What's a pauper's grave?'

Palmer explained. 'The local council has a legal duty to bury anybody who has no relatives and no means of payment. Usually it's a cremation these days, so I expect the residents may have had a whip round to upgrade this one.'

'Have you seen Motörhead, guv?' Gheeta was smiling. 'I hardly recognised her.'

Palmer looked along the lines of mourners. 'Can't see her, where is she?'

'Third from the left, in the row nearest the graves.'

Palmer found her. 'You're kidding. Is that her?

'Yes.'

Motörhead had obviously had a hell of a make-over. She no longer looked like a refugee from a charity shop. The hair was blue like the other ladies, but with flicks of blonde and professionally added extensions to make it reach her shoulders. The overcoat and purple trouser suit were obviously expensive, as was the Burberry shoulder bag and Tommy Hilfiger knit heel boots.

'It must be a twin.' Palmer could hardly believe the transformation.

'Don't think so, guv. Do you think there's a Motörhead T-shirt under that jacket?'

'I doubt it. High heels as well – she wants to be careful or she'll go headfirst into one of the graves.'

'Does '*mutton dressed as lamb*' come to mind, guv?'

'Definitely, but I bet nobody dares say it to her face. I can see Cathy and her kids as well, they look normal. Either of you two see Samantha?'

They couldn't.

'I don't think she'd take a chance and be here, sir, 'said Knight. 'She knows we are looking for her.'

They waited as the ceremony drew to a close and the mourners slowly walked past them towards the road and the public car park. Some smiled, most ignored, and a few glared. Motörhead was with Cathy and the children; she recognised Palmer and came over, her lungs already pumping on a cigarette in her mouth.

'Mr Palmer, didn't expect to see you here.' She noticed his crutch, 'What have you done?'

'Slight accident, Mrs Johnson, nothing too serious. Looks like the local hairdresser had a run on blue rinses. We thought we'd pay our respects.'

'Rubbish, don't give me that – you thought Sammy might be here. Maybe she was.' She laughed, before her expression turned serious. 'I see you've got the two bastards who did it then – hope they go away for life.'

'I've a feeling they might, Mrs Johnson, they well might.'

'Good.' She nodded and walked away; then, remembering something, turned back towards them. 'By the way, Cathy and me is moving, so don't come round the Bevan if you're looking for us.'

'Really, where are you going?'

'A long way away.' She turned and walked away.

'She must be doing a council swap with somebody,' Gheeta said. 'Can't blame her and Cathy for wanting to get away from those memories. I'll get her new address off the council housing department in case we need her as a witness.'

Knight nodded towards the graves. 'Look at that – didn't take long, did it?'

They looked to where the digger was already dumping earth in the last of the three graves and smoothing it over. The gravedigger looked their way and recognised Gheeta with a wave. She waved back.

'I'll just pop over and say hello, guv. I'd better warn him too, he might be called to court as well.'

She walked over as Palmer and Knight waited. After a brief conversation Gheeta beckoned them to join her, which they did.

'This is interesting, guv – head groundsman (they don't like being called gravediggers) says there are three gravestones being delivered tomorrow. One for each of the boys and all inscribed with their names, dates of birth and death, and a message on each saying *'Gone but never forgotten.'*

'From the council?' Palmer hadn't come across the council doing that before.

'I don't think so, guv – the chap here says they are rose colour Indian Granite. Expensive.'

'Eight hundred quid each minimum,' added the groundsman. 'Plus the engraving.'

Palmer looked at Knight. 'Samantha.'

'Yes, got to be using some of the money from Day's bank account.'

'Only some of it,' said Gheeta. 'She's starting to spend it – no wonder her mum looked smart.'

'Yes, but as you say, Sergeant, only some of it – the stones would hardly make a dent in eight hundred thousand.'

'I think I might go over to the Bevan estate, sir, and have a nose round,' said Knight. 'Might be a small wake going on, and with a bit of luck Samantha will show up.'

'Good idea, Knight,' Palmer agreed.

****

The driver dropped Palmer and Singh off at the Yard and went onto the Bevan estate with Knight.

In less than an hour he was back, walking into the Team Room with a disconsolate look on his face.

'They've gone.'

'Who's gone?' asked Palmer.

'Motörhead and Cathy, both flats are empty. There's a code of silence amongst the neighbours, nobody knows where they've gone. They probably do, but they're not saying, and I noticed a certain amount of new kids' bikes, new curtains at windows, mothers with spanking new prams, and they've all got video doorbells now.'

'Samantha's been splashing the cash, buying silence – clever girl.' Palmer had to admit his admiration of Samantha was growing all the time. He looked at Claire. 'Claire, give the local council housing department a ring and see where they've gone.'

Gheeta could see what the answer would be. 'They won't know, guv – it Motörhead and Cathy had done swaps with other council tenants, the new tenants would be in by now, wouldn't they? The flats wouldn't be empty like Knight says they are.'

'Of course.' Palmer could see the logic. 'Give the council a ring in any case, Claire, see if they can throw any light on where they've gone. They may have a forwarding address – same for the post office and utilities. One of them may know.'

They didn't. The council couldn't help as both Motörhead and Cathy had paid up any rent arrears, moved out and off the council list. As Gheeta had said, they didn't do swaps. The utilities were the same; both had been on pre-paid meters, so no need for a forwarding address for any bills.

Claire rang the local school. Cathy's children hadn't been in for three days; she had phoned the secretary and told her they wouldn't be back as she was going to home educate them. Nothing the school could do except register the fact with the local education authority who would visit to monitor the situation, but that wouldn't be for a few weeks and Cathy was already gone. With Day's money the children were probably enrolled in the '*no questions asked for cash*' private school system somewhere. The trail was cold.

****

THE AFTERMATH

The next March was warm. Palmer liked the spring, time of new beginnings, new growth in the garden, except the Aster bed, and a new fence panel. A clean sheet and all the expectation of a good summer to come. The plaster cast was off replaced by bandage strapping as the break had set leaving Palmer with just a slight limp which he disguised as much as he could. He had removed his jacket as he sat on the public benches in Court One of the Old Bailey and gave Gheeta and Knight sitting either side of him a broad satisfied smile as the Judge sent Black and Houseman down for three concurrent life terms each, plus a non parole stipulation. That would go forward to the Home Secretary who would add a full life tariff as is the practice in such cases. Black and Houseman would die in prison. The CPS prosecutor looked up at Palmer from the court floor and they gave each other a smile and a nod that said *'job done'*.

In the corridor outside the courtroom, Lucy Price shepherded the three of them, together with the prosecutor and AC Bateman, to wait until the public had left before facing the assembled press outside. Bateman straightened his tie and took a tissue from his pocket to wipe

211

over his head whilst running the speech he had rehearsed in his office mirror ten times through his mind once more.

The media and their journalists and cameras swamped the pavement outside The Old Bailey Court Number One public entrance. Television satellite vans waited on the road, the producers inside priming the anchors back in the studios to be ready to interrupt the news programmes at short notice.

Lucy led them out and silenced the plethora of questions being shouted with a wave of her hands. Silence fell and the CPS prosecutor stepped forward and spoke.

She said how the case had been the most awful serial killer case in her career, and praised the SMS and Chief Superintendent Palmer for their work in bringing Black and Houseman to justice.

Palmer had told Lucy that he wouldn't take questions; not his style, leave it to Bateman.

Bateman took the questions and Palmer's mind drifted off, he was hoping the media interest would die down quickly as after every case that made the headlines his neighbours would want to talk to him about it when he took Daisy round the park or Mrs P. shopping, or even just when they saw him in his garden; and of course he had to be polite as he answered the same questions for the tenth time.

He glanced at the journalists; many he knew by name and had built up a good relationship with over the years. One he didn't recognise was stood to the side of the crowd at the back, a young person in jeans and a hoodie who seemed to be staring at him and not making notes like the others were as Bateman rambled on. He looked away and then back again; the person's attention was definitely on him and only him. He gave a slight smile. The smile was returned as the person raised a hand and slipped the hoodie off. Bright blue hair gave the game away. Samantha Johnson nodded and mouthed *'thank you'* before pulling the hoodie back up and disappearing behind the crowd.

THE END

Thank you for buying this book. If you enjoyed it please leave a review or rating on Amazon as that would mean an awful lot to me. Thank you.

To see more books in this series and others, and to get updates on new releases check my website:

www.barry-faulkner.com

Whilst there you may also like to sign up to my newsletter and receive advance notice of new books, freebies, talks, Literary Festivals I attend and other interesting posts. You can unsubscribe at any time and it's all **FREE**!!

Take care and stay safe!

DCS Palmer books
Future Riches
The Felt Tip Murders
A Killer is Calling
Poetic Justice
Loot
I'm With The Band
Burning Ambition
Take Away Terror
Ministry of Death

The Bodybuilder
Succession
The Black Rose
Laptops Can Kill

**Ben Nevis and the Gold Digger
Series**
Turkish Delight
National Treasure

London Crime 1930s-2021 (factual)
UK Serial Killers 1930-2021 (factual)

Bidder Beware (Comedy crime)
Fred Karno   biography

www.barry-faulkner.com

Printed in Great Britain
by Amazon